# True Love

# True Love

## A Story of English Domestic Life

Sarah E. Farro

MINT EDITIONS

*True Love: A Story of English Domestic Life* was first published in 1859.

This edition published by Mint Editions 2021.

ISBN 9781513282633 | E-ISBN 9781513287652

Published by Mint Editions®

 MINT
EDITIONS

minteditionbooks.com

Publishing Director: Jennifer Newens
Design & Production: Rachel Lopez Metzger
Project Manager: Micaela Clark
Typesetting: Westchester Publishing Services

# Contents

# Preface

The author is aware that she is entering a field which has been diligently cultivated by the best minds in Europe and America. Her design in the preparation of this story is to give to the public a sketch of her ideas on the effect of "true love." I have tried to make the plot exciting without being sensational or common, although within the bounds of proper romance, and create a set of characters most of whom are like real people with whose thoughts and passions we are able to sympathize and whose language and conduct may be appreciable or reprehensible according to circumstances. Great pains have been taken to make this work superior in its arrangement and finish and in the general tastefulness of its mechanical execution. How nearly the author has accomplished her purpose to give to the public in one volume a clear and complete treatise on this subject, combining many fine qualities of importance to the reader, the intelligent and experienced public must decide.

Sarah E. Farro

# I

## Mrs. Brewster's Daughters

A fine old door of oak, a heavy door standing deep within a portico inside of which you might have driven a coach, brings you to the residence of Mrs. Brewster. The hall was dark and small, the only light admitted to it being from windows of stained glass; numberless passages branched off from the hall, one peculiarity being that you could scarcely enter a single room in it but you must first go down a passage, short or long, to get to it; had the house been designed by an architect with a head upon his shoulders and a little common sense within it, he might have made a respectable house to say the least; as it was, the rooms were cramped and narrow, cornered and confined, and the good space was taken up by these worthless passages; a plat of ground before it was crowded with flowers, far too crowded for good taste, as the old gardener would point out to her, but Mrs. Brewster loved flowers and would not part with one of them. Being the daughter of a carpenter and the wife of a merchant tailor, she had scrambled through life amidst bustle and poverty, moving from one house to another, never settled anywhere for long. It was an existence not to be envied, although it is the lot of many. She was Mrs. Brewster and her husband was not a very good husband to her; he was rather too fond of amusing himself, and threw all the care upon her shoulders; she spent her time nursing her sickly children and endeavouring to make one dollar go as far as two. One day, to her unspeakable embarrassment, she found herself changed from a poor woman in moderate circumstances to an heiress to a certain degree, her father having received a legacy from a relative, and upon his death it was willed to her. She had much sorrow, having lost one child after another, until she had but two left. Then she lost her husband and father; then settled at Bellville near her husband's native place, upon her limited means. All she possessed was the interest upon this sum her father had left her, the whole not exceeding $2,000. She had two daughters, Mary Ann and Janey; the contrast between them was great, you could see it most remarkably as they sat together, and her love for them was as contrasted as light is with darkness. Mary Ann she regarded with an inordinate affection amounting almost to a passion; for Janey she did not care; what could be the reason of this; what is the reason that parents, many such may be found, will love some of their children and dislike others they cannot tell any more than she could; ask them and they will be unable to give you an answer. It does not lie in the children; it often happens that those obtaining the least love will be the most deserving of it. Such was the case here. Mary Ann Brewster was a pale, sickly, fretful girl, full of whims, full of complaints, giving trouble to everybody about her. Janey, with her sweet countenance and her merry heart, made the sunshine of her home; she bore with her sister's exacting moods, she bore with her mother's want of love, she loved them both and waited on them, and carrolled forth her snatches of song as she moved around the house, and was as happy as the day was long. Ask the servants—they kept only two—and they would tell you that Mrs. Brewster was cross and selfish, but Miss Janey was worth her weight in gold; the gold was soon to be transplanted to a home where it would be appreciated and cherished, for Janey was the affianced wife of Charles Taylor. For nearly a mile beyond Bellville lived Charles Taylor, a quiet, refined gentleman, and the son of a wealthy capitalist; his father had not only made a fortune of his own, but had several bestowed upon him; he had died several years before this time, and his wife survived him one year. There were three sisters, a cousin and two servants that had lived in this family for a number of years.

The beams of the setting sun streamed into the dining-room of the Taylor mansion; it was a room of fine proportions, not dull and heavy as it is the custom of some dining-rooms, but light and graceful as could be wished. Charles Taylor, with his fine beauty, sat at one end of the room, Miss Mary Taylor, a maiden lady of mature years, good looking also in her peculiar style, sat opposite him, she wore a white dress, its make remarkably young, and her hair fell in ringlets, young also; at her right-hand sat Matilda, singularly attractive in her quiet loveliness, with her silver dotted muslin dress trimmed with white ribbons; at her left sat Martha, quiet in manner, plain in features; she had large gray eyes, reflective strangely deep, with a circle of darker gray around them, when they were cast upon you it was not at you they looked, but at what was within you, at your mind, your thoughts; at least such was the impression they carried. Thus sat this worthy group, deep in thought, for they had been conversing about the weather, that had been so damp, for it had been raining for months, and the result was a malarial fever, visiting the residents of Bellville, and it was very dangerous, for the sufferer would soon lapse into unconsciousness and all was over; and it was generally believed that the fever was abated. A rap at the door brought Charles Taylor to his feet, it was George, the old gardener, he had come to tell them the fever had broken out again. "What!" exclaimed Charles. "The fever broken out again?" "Yes, it have," said George, who had the build of a Dutchman, and was taciturn upon most subjects; in manner he was most surly and would hold his own opinion, especially if it touched upon his occupation, against the world.

The news fell upon Charles' heart like a knell; he fully believed the danger to have passed, though not yet the sickness. "Are you sure that the fever has broken out again, George?" he asked, after a pause. "I ain't no surer than I was told," returned George. "I met Doctor Brown, and he said as he passed, that the fever had broken out again." "Do you know where?" asked Charles. "He said, I believe, but I didn't catch it; if I stopped to listen to the talk of fevers where would my work be?" George moved on ere he had done speaking, possibly from the impression that the present talk was not forwarding his work. Taking his black silk hat Charles said, "I shall go out and see if I can glean any news; I hope it may be a false report." He was just outside the walks when he saw Doctor Brown, the most popular doctor in the village, coming along quickly in his buggy; Charles motioned his hand, and the driver pulled up. "Is it true, this fresh report of fever?" "Too true, I fear," replied the doctor. "I am on my way now, just summoned." "Who's attacked?" "Mary Ann Brewster." The name appeared to startle Charles. "Mary Ann Brewster," he uttered, "she will never pull through it." The doctor raised his eye-brows as if he thought it doubtful, and motioned to his driver to move on. On the morning in question Mary Ann Brewster awoke sick; in her impatient, fretful way she called out to Janey, who slept in an adjoining room. Janey was fast asleep, but she was used to being aroused out of her sleep at unreasonable hours by Mary Ann and she threw on her dressing-gown and hastened to her. "I want some tea," began Mary Ann, "I am as sick and thirsty as I can be." She was really of a sickly constitution and to hear her complain of being "sick and thirsty" was nothing unusual. Janey in her loving nature, her sweet patience, received the information with as much concern as though she had never heard it before. She bent over Mary Ann and spoke tenderly, "where do you feel pain, dear, in your head or chest, where is it?" "I told you that I was sick and thirsty, and that's enough," peevishly answered Mary Ann. "Go and get me some tea." "As soon as I can," said Janey, soothingly. "There is no fire yet, the girls are not up, I do not think it can be later than four, by the look of the morning." "Very well," cried Mary Ann, the sobs being contrived by the catching up of her breath in temper not by tears, "you can't call the maids I suppose, and you can't put yourself the least out of the way to alleviate my suffering; you want to go to bed again and sleep till nine o'clock; when I am dead you will wish you were more like a sister; you possess great, rude health yourself, and you feel no compassion for those who do not." An assertion unjust and untrue like many others made by Mary Ann. Janey did not possess rude health, though she was not like her sister always complaining, and she had more compassion for Mary Ann than she deserved. "I will see what I can do," she gently said, "you shall soon have some tea." Passing into her own room Janey hastily dressed herself. When Mary Ann was in one of her exacting moods there could be no more sleep for Janey.

"I wonder," she said to herself, "whether I could not make the fire without waking the girls, they had such a hard day's work yesterday cleaning house; yes, if I can get some chips I will make a fire." She went down to the kitchen, hunted up what was required, laid the fire and lighted it; it did not burn quickly, she thought the chips might be damp and she got the bellows; there she was on her knees blowing at the chips and sending the blaze amid the coals, when some one entered the kitchen. "Miss Janey!" It was one of the girls, Eliza; she had heard a noise in the kitchen and had arisen. Janey explained that her sister was sick and tea was wanted. "Why did you not call us?" "You went to bed so late and had worked so hard, I thought that I would not disturb you." "But it is not lady's work, Miss." "I think ladies should put on gloves when they undertake it," gayly laughed Janey; "look at my black hands." "What would Mr. Taylor say if he saw you on your knees lighting a fire?" "He would say I was doing right, Eliza," replied Janey, a shade of reproof in her firm tones, though the allusion caused the color to crimson her cheeks; the girl had been with them some time and assumed more privilege than a less respected servant would have been allowed to do. The tea ready Janey carried a cup of it to her sister, with a slice of toast that she had made. Mary Ann drank the tea at a draught, but she turned with a shiver from the toast, she seemed to be shivering much. "Who was so stupid as to make that? you might know I could not eat it, I am too sick." Janey began to think she looked very sick, her face was flushed shivering though she was, her lips were dry, her bright eyes were unnaturally heavy; she gently laid her hands, cleanly

SARAH E. FARRO

washed, upon her sister's brow; it felt burning, and Mary Ann screamed out, "Do keep your hands away, my head is splitting with pain." All at once Janey thought of the fever, the danger from which they had been reckoning to have passed. "Would you like me to bathe your forehead with water, Mary Ann?" asked Janey, kindly. "I would like you to stop until things are asked for and not to worry me," replied Mary Ann. Janey sighed, not for the cross temper, Mary Ann was always cross in sickness, but for the suffering she thought she saw and the half-doubt, half-dread which had arisen within her. I think I had better call mamma, she thought to herself, though if she sees nothing unusual the matter with Mary Ann she will only be angry with me; proceeding to her mother's chamber Janey knocked gently, her mother slept still, but the entrance aroused her. "Mamma, I do not like to disturb you, but Mary Ann is sick." "Sick again, and only last week she was in bed three days, poor, dear sufferer; is it her chest?"

"Mamma she seems unusually ill, otherwise I should not have disturbed you, I feared, I thought you will be angry with me, if I say, perhaps;" "say what, don't stand like a statue, Janey." Janey dropped her voice, "dear mamma, suppose it should be the fever?" For one startling moment Mrs. Brewster felt as if a dagger was piercing her heart; the next she turned upon Janey. "Fever for Mary Ann! How dared she prophesy it, a low common fever confined to the poor and the town and which had gone away or all but; was it likely to turn itself back again and come up here to attack her darling child?" Janey, the tears in her eyes, said she hoped it would prove to be only a common headache; that it was her love for Mary Ann which awoke her fears. The mother proceeded to the sick-chamber and Janey followed. Mrs. Brewster was not accustomed to observe caution and she spoke freely of the "fever" before Mary Ann; seemingly for the purpose of casting blame upon Janey. Mary Ann did not catch the fear, she ridiculed Janey as her mother had done; for several hours Mrs. Brewster did not catch it either, she would have summoned medical aid at first, but Mary Ann in her fretfulness protested that she would not have a doctor; later she grew worse and Doctor Brown was sent for, you saw him in his buggy going to the house.

Mrs. Brewster came forward to meet him, Janey, full of anxiety, near her. Mrs. Brewster was a thin woman, with a shriveled face and a sharp red nose, her gray hair banded closely under a white cap, her style of head-dress never varied, it consisted always of a plain cap with a quilled border trimmed with purple ribbon, her black dresses she had not laid aside since the death of her husband and intended never to do so. She grasped the arm of the doctor, "You must save my child!" "Higher aid permitting me," answered the surgeon. "What makes you think it's the fever? For months I have been summoned by timid parents to any number of fever cases and when I have arrived in haste they have turned out to be no fever at all." "This is the fever," Mrs. Brewster replied; "had I been more willing to admit that it was, you would have been sent for hours ago, it was Janey's fault; she suggested at daybreak that it might be the fever, and it made my darling girl so angry that she forbade my sending for advice; but she is worse now, come and see her." The doctor laid his hand upon Janey's head with a fond gesture as he followed Mrs. Brewster; all the neighbors of Bellville loved Janey Brewster. Tossing upon her uneasy bed, her face crimson, her hair floating untidily around it, lay Mary Ann, still shivering; the doctor gave one glance at her, it was quite enough to satisfy him that the mother was not mistaken.

"Is it the fever," impatiently asked Mary Ann, unclosing her hot eyelids; "if it is we must drive it away," said the doctor cheerfully. "Why should the fever have come to me?" she rejoined in a tone of rebellion. "Why was I thrown from my buggy last year and my back sprained? Such unpleasant things do come to us." "To sprain your back is nothing compared with this fever; you got well again." "And we will get you well if you will be quiet and reasonable." "I am so hot, my head is so heavy." The doctor, who had called for water and a glass, was mixing up a brown powder which he had produced from his pocket; she drank it without opposition, and then he lessened the weight of the bed-clothes, and afterwards turned his attention to the bed-room. It was close and hot, and the sun which had just burst forth brightly from the gray sky shone full upon it. "You have got the chimney stuffed up," he exclaimed. "Mary Ann will not allow it to be open," said Mrs. Brewster; "she is sensitive to cold, and feels the slightest draught." The doctor walked to the chimney, turned up his coat cuff and wristband and pulled down a bag filled with shavings; some soot came with it and covered his hand, but he did not mind that; he was as little given to ceremony as Mrs. Brewster was to caution, and he walked leisurely up to the wash-stand to wash it off. "Now, if I catch that bag or any other bag up there obstructing the air, I shall pull down the bricks and make a good big hole that the sky can be seen through; of that I give you notice, madam."

He next pulled the window down at the top behind the blind, but the room at its best did not find favor with him. "It is not airy; it is not cool," he said. "Is there not a better ventilated room in the house? if so, she shall be moved to it." "My room is a cool one," interposed Janey eagerly; "the sun never shines upon it, doctor." It appears that Janey, thus speaking, must have reminded the doctor that she was present for in the same unceremonious fashion that he had laid his hands upon the chimney bag, he now laid them upon her shoulder and walked her out of the room. "You go down stairs, Miss Janey, and do not come within a mile of this room again until I give you notice." During this time Mary Ann was talking imperiously and fretfully. "I will not be moved into Janey's room; it is not furnished with half the comforts of mine; it has only a little bed-side carpet; I will not go there, doctor." "Now, see here, Mary Ann," said the doctor firmly, "I am responsible for getting you well, and I shall take my own way to do it. If I am to be contradicted at every suggestion, your mother can summon some one else to attend you, I will not undertake it."

"My dear you shall not be moved to Janey's room;" said her mother coaxingly; "you shall be moved to mine, it is larger than this, you know, doctor, with a draught through it, if you wish to open the door and windows."

"Very well," replied the doctor, "let me find her in it when I come again this evening, and if there's a carpet on the floor take it up, carpets were never intended for bed-rooms." He went into one of the sitting-rooms with Mrs. Brewster as he descended; "What do you think of the case," she earnestly inquired. "There will be some difficulty with it," was his candid reply. "Her hair must be cut off." "Her hair cut off!" screamed Mrs. Brewster, "that it never shall! She has the most beautiful hair, what is Janey's compared to her's?"

"You heard what I said," he positively replied.

"But Mary Ann will not allow it to be done," she returned, shifting the ground of remonstrance from her own shoulders, "and to do it in opposition would be enough to kill her." "It will not be done in opposition," he answered, "she will be unconscious before it is attempted." Mrs. Brewster's heart sank within her. "You anticipate she will be dangerously ill?" "In such cases there is always danger, but worse cases than, as I believe hers will be, are curable." "If I lose her I shall die myself," she exclaimed, "and if she is to have it badly she will die! Remember, doctor, how weak she has always been." "We sometimes find that the weak of constitution battle best with an epidemic," he replied, "many a hearty one is stricken down with it and taken off, many a sickly one has pulled through it and been the better afterwards."

"Everything shall be done as you wish," said Mrs. Brewster humbly in her great fear. "Very well. There is one caution I would earnestly impress upon you, that of keeping Janey from the sick-room." "But there is no one to whom Mary Ann is so accustomed as a nurse," objected Mrs. Brewster. "Madam," burst forth the doctor angrily, "would you subject Janey to the risk of taking the infection in deference to Mary Ann's selfishness or to yours, better lose all the treasures your house contains than lose Janey, she is the greatest treasure." "I know how remarkably prejudiced you have always been in Janey's favor," spitefully spoke Mrs. Brewster. "If I disliked her as much as I like her, I should be equally solicitous to guard her from the danger of infection," said Doctor Brown. "If you chose to put Janey out of consideration you cannot put Charles Taylor; in justice to him she must be taken care of."

Mrs. Brewster opened her mouth to reply, but closed it again; strange words had been hovering upon her lips. "If Charles Taylor had not been blind his choice would have fallen upon Mary Ann, not upon Janey." In her heart there was a sore topic of resentment; for she fully appreciated the advantages of a union with the Taylors. Those words were swallowed down to give utterance to others. "Janey is in the house, and therefore must be liable to take the fever; whether she takes the infection or not, I cannot fence her around with an air-tight wall so that not a breath of tainted atmosphere shall touch her, I would if I could, but I cannot." "I would send her from the house, Mrs. Brewster; at any rate, I would forbid her to go near her sister; I don't want two patients on my hands instead of one," he added in his quaint fashion as he took his departure. He was about to step into his buggy when he saw Charles Taylor advancing with a quick step. "Which of them is it that is seized?" he inquired as he came up. "Not Janey, thank goodness," replied the doctor. "It is Mary Ann; I have been persuading the madam to send Janey from home; I should send her were she a daughter of mine." "Is Mary Ann likely to have it dangerously?" "I think she will. Is there any necessity for you going to the house just now, Mr. Taylor?" Charles Taylor smiled. "There is no necessity for my keeping away; I do not fear the fever any more than you do." He passed into the garden as he spoke, and the doctor drove on. Janey saw him and came running out. "Oh! Charles, don't come in; do not come." His only answer was to take her upon his arm and enter. He raised the drawing-room window, that as much air might circulate through the house as was possible, and stood at it with her holding her before him. "Janey, what am I to do with you?" "To do with me? What should you do with me, Charles?" "Do you know, my dear, that I cannot afford to let this danger touch you?" "I am not afraid," she gently said. He knew that she had a brave unselfish heart, but he was afraid for her, for he loved her with a jealous love, jealous of any evil that might come too near her. "I should like to take you out of the house with me now, Janey. I should like to take you far from this fever-tainted town; will you come?" She looked up at him with a smile, the color coming into her cheeks. "How could I, Charles?" Anxious thoughts were passing through the mind of Charles Taylor. We cannot put aside the conventionalities of life, though there are times when they press upon us as an iron weight; he would have given his own life almost to have taken Janey from that house, but how was he to do it? No friend would be likely to receive her; not even his own sisters; they would have too much dread of the infection she might bring. He would fain have carried her to some sea-breezed town and watch over her and guard her there until the danger should be over. None would have protected her more honorably than Charles Taylor. But those conventionalities the world has to bow down to, how would the step have accorded with them? Another thought passed through his mind. "Listen, Janey," he said, "suppose we get a license and drive to the parson's house; it could all be done in a few hours, and you could be away with me before night." As the meaning dawned upon her, she bent her head, and her blushing face, laughing at the wild improbability. "Oh! Charles, you are only joking; what would people say?" "Would it make any difference to us what they said?" "It could not be, Charles; it is a vision impossible," she replied seriously. "Were all other things meet, how could I run away from my sister on her bed of dangerous illness to marry you?"

Janey was right and Charles Taylor felt that she was; the conventionalities must be observed no matter at what cost. He held her fondly against his heart, "if aught of ill should arise to you from your remaining here I should never forgive myself." Charles could not remain longer, he must be at his office, for business was urging. His cousin, George Gay, was in the private room alone when he entered, he appeared to be buried five feet deep in business, though he would have preferred to be five feet deep in pleasure. "Are you going home to supper this evening?" inquired Charles. "The fates permitting," replied

Mr. Gay, "You tell my sisters that I will not return until after tea, Mary will not thank me for running from Mrs. Brewster's house to hers, just now." "Charles," warmly spoke George in an impulse of kindly feeling, "I do hope the fever will not extend itself to Janey." "I hope not," fervently breathed Charles Taylor.

## II

## THE RESIDENCE OF CHARLES TAYLOR

In the heart of Bellville was situated the business house of Bangs, Smith & Taylor, built at the corner of a street, it faced two ways, the office and its doors being on L street, the principal street of the town. There was also a dwelling-house on M street, a new short street not much frequented. There were eight or ten houses on this street all owned by the Taylors, and this street led to the open country and to a carriage way that would take you to the Taylor mansion. It was in one of these houses that Charles Taylor had concluded to live after his marriage with Janey Brewster, as it was near his business and he wanted his sisters to live there with him as it was their mother's last request that they keep together, but up to the present time he had never talked the matter over with them. This house attached to the office was a commodious one, its rooms were mostly large and handsome and many in number, a pillared entrance to which you ascended by steps took you into a large hall, on the right of this hall was a room used for a dining-room, a light and spacious apartment, its large window opening on a covered terrace where plants could be kept and that again standing open to a sloping lawn surrounded with shrubs and flowers. On the left of the hall was a kitchen, pantries and such like, at the back of the hall beyond the dining-room a handsome staircase led to the apartments, one of which was a fine drawing-room. From the upper windows at the back of the house a full view of the Taylor mansion might be obtained, rising high and picturesque, also the steeple of a cathedral gray and grim, not of the cathedral itself, its surrounding trees concealed that.

In the dining-room of the Taylor mansion one evening sat Charles Taylor and his eldest sister, Mary. This room was elegant and airy and fitted up with exquisite taste; it was the ladies' favorite sitting-room. The drawing-room above was larger and grander but less used by them. On the evening in question, Charles Taylor was arranging plans for a business trip with his sister, though her removal to town was uppermost in his mind. About ten days previous to this, Marshall Bangs, one of the partners, had been found insensible on the floor of his room; he was subject to attacks of heart-disease, and this had proved to be nothing but a fainting spell, but it had caused plans to be somewhat changed, for Mr. Bangs would not be strong enough for business consultation, which would have been the chief object of his journey. As I said before, Charles and his sister were sitting alone, their cousin, George Gay, had gone out for a walk and Martha was spending the evening at Parson Davis', for she and Mrs. Davis were active workers in church affairs. The dessert was on the table, but Charles had turned from it and was sitting opposite the fireplace. Miss Taylor sat opposite him, nearer the table, her fingers busy with knitting, on which fell the rays of the chandelier. "Mary," said Charles, earnestly, "I wish that you would let me bring Janey here on a visit to you." Mary laid down her knitting. "What, do you mean that there should be two mistresses in the house, she and I? No, Charles, the daftest old wife in all the world would tell you that would not do." "Not two mistresses; you would be sole mistress, as you are now; Janey and I your guests, indeed Mary, it would be the best plan. Suppose we all move to town together," he said. "It was mother's desire that we should remain together." "No, Charles, it would not do; some of the partners have always resided near the office, and it is necessary, in my opinion, that you should let business men be at their business. When do you contemplate marrying Janey," she inquired, after a few minutes of thought. "I should like her to be mine by Thanksgiving," was the low answer. "Charles! and November close upon us." "If not, some time in December," he continued, paying no heed to her surprise. "It is so decided." Miss Taylor drew a long breath. "With whom is it decided?" "With Janey." "You marry a wife without a home to bring her too; had cousin George told me that he was going to do such a thing I would have believed him, not of you, Charles!" "Mary, the home shall no longer be a barrier. I wish you would receive Janey here as your guest."

"It is not likely that she would come; the first thing a married woman looks out for is a home of her own."

Charles laughed. "Not come? Mary, have you yet to learn how unassuming and meek is the character of Janey? We have spoken of this plan together, and Janey's only fear is lest she should be in the way of Miss Taylor failing in the carrying out of this project. Mary (for I see you are as I thought you would be, prejudiced against it) I shall take one of the houses near the office in town and there I shall take Janey. The pleasantest plan would be for me to bring Janey here, entirely as your guest; it is what she and I would both like. If you object, I shall take her elsewhere."

Mary knitted a whole row before she spoke. "I will take a few days to reflect upon it, Charles," she said. "Do so," he replied, rising and glancing at his watch. "Half past eight. What time will Martha expect me? I wish to spend half an hour with Janey, shall I go for Martha before or afterwards?"

"Go for her at once, Charles; it will be better for her to be home early."

Charles Taylor went to the hall door and looked out upon the night; he was considering whether he need put on an overcoat. It was a bright moonlight night, pleasant and genial, so he closed the door and started. "I wish the cold would come," he exclaimed half aloud; he was thinking of the fever which still clung to Bellville, showing itself fitfully and partially in fresh places about every three or four days. He took the path leading to L. street, a lonely road and at night unfrequented; the pathway was so narrow that two people could scarcely walk abreast without touching the trunks of the maple trees growing on either side and meeting overhead. Charles Taylor went steadily on, his thoughts running upon the subject of his conversation with Mary.

It is probable that but for the difficulty touching a residence, Janey would have been his the past summer. Altogether, Charles' plan was the best, if Mary could be brought to see it, that his young bride should be her guest for a short time. Charles, in due course of time, arrived at the walk's end and passed through a large gate. The town lay in front of him, gray and sombre, as it was nearly hidden by trees; he looked at it fondly, his heart yearned to it, for it was to be the future home of Janey and himself.

"Hello! who's there? Oh, I beg your pardon, Mr. Taylor."

The speaker was Doctor Brown. He had come swiftly upon Charles Taylor, turning from the corner around the maple trees; that he had been to see the sick was certain, but Charles had not heard of any one being sick in that direction. "Neither had I," said the doctor, in answer to the remark, "until I was sent for an hour ago in haste." A thought crossed Charlie's mind, "Not a case of fever, I hope." "No; I think that's leaving us. There's been an accident to the parson's wife—at least what might have been an accident, I should rather say," added the doctor, correcting himself; "the injury is so slight as not to be worth the name of one." "What has happened?" asked Charles Taylor. "She managed to set her sleeve on fire. A muslin, falling over the merino sleeve of her gown, in standing near a candle, the flame caught it; but just look at her presence of mind! Instead of wasting time running through the house from top to bottom, as most of them would have done, she instantly threw herself down on the rug and rolled herself into it. She's the kind of a woman to go through life." "Is she much burnt?" "No; many a child gets more burnt a dozen times in its first dozen years. The arm, between the elbow and wrist, is a little scorched; it's nothing; they need not have sent for me; a drop of cold water applied will take out all the fire. Your sister Martha was much more frightened than she was." "I'm really glad it's no worse," said Charles Taylor. "I feared the fever might have broken out again." "That is taking its departure, I think, and the sooner it's gone the better; it has been capricious as a coquette's smiles; it is strange that in many houses it should have attacked only one inmate and spared the rest." "What do you think, now, of Mary Ann Brewster?" The doctor shook his head, and his voice grew insensibly low. "In my opinion, she is sinking fast. I found her worse this afternoon, weaker than she has been at all; her mother thought that if she could get her to Newtown she might improve; but the removal would kill her; she would die on the road. It will be a terrible blow to her mother if it does come; and, though it may be harsh to say it, a retort upon her selfishness. Did you hear that she used to make Janey head nurse while the fever was upon her?" "No," exclaimed Charles Taylor. "They did, though; Mrs. Brewster let it out to-day unintentionally. Dear girl! if she had caught it, I should never have forgiven her mother, whatever you may have done. I have a few more visits to make now before bedtime. Good-night!"

"Worse!" exclaimed Charles, as he walked on, "poor Mary Ann, but I wonder"—he hesitated as the thought struck him whether if the worse should come, as the doctor seems to anticipate, if it would delay Janey's marriage, what with one delay and another. He walked on to the parson's house where he found Mrs. Davis, playing the invalid, lying on a sofa, her auburn hair was disheveled, her cheeks flushed; the burnt arm, her muslin sleeve pinned up, was stretched out on a cushion, a pocket handkerchief, saturated with water, resting lightly on the burns, a basin of water stood near with another handkerchief in it, and the maid was near to exchange the handkerchiefs as might be required. Charles Taylor drew his chair near to Mrs. Davis and listened to the account of the accident, giving her his full sympathy, for it might have been a bad one. "You must possess great presence of mind," he observed. "I think your showing it, as you have done in this instance, has won the doctor's heart." Mrs. Davis smiled. "I believe I do possess presence of mind; once we were riding out with some friends in a carriage when the horses took fright, ran away, and nearly tore the carriage to pieces; while all were frightened in a fearful manner I remained calm and cool." "It is a good thing for you," he observed. "I suppose it is; better at any rate than to go mad with fear, as some do. Martha has had enough fright to last her for a year." "What were you doing, Martha?" asked her brother. "I was present but I did not see it," replied Martha; "it occurred in her room, and I was in the hall looking out of the window with my back to her; the first I knew or saw, Mrs. Davis was lying on the floor with the rug rolled around her." Tea was brought in and Mrs. Davis insisted that they should remain to it. Charles pleaded an engagement but she would not listen; they could not have the heart to leave her alone, so Charles, the very essence of good feeling and politeness, remained. Tea having been over, Martha went upstairs to get her wraps. Mrs. Davis turned her head as the door was closed and then spoke abruptly: "I am glad that Mr. Davis was not here, he would have magnified it into something formidable, and I should not have been let stir for a month." The door opened, Martha appeared, they wished Mrs. Davis "good night," a speedy cure from her burns, and departed, Charles, taking the straight path this time, which did not lead them near the maple trees. "How quaint old Doctor Brown is," said Martha, as they walked along; "when he had looked at Mrs. Davis' arm he made a great parade of getting out his glasses and putting them on, and looking again."

"What do you call it, a burn?" he asked her. "It is a burn, is it not," she answered, looking at him. "No," said he, "its nothing but a singe," it made her laugh heartily. "I guess she was pleased to have escaped with such slight damage." "That is just like Doctor Brown," said Charles.

Having arrived at home, Miss Taylor was in the same place knitting still; it was half past ten, too late for Charles to pay a visit to Mrs. Brewster. "Mary, I fear you have waited tea for us," said Martha. "To be sure child, I expected you home to it."

Martha explained why she did not come, telling of the accident to Mrs. Davis. "Ah, careless! careless! careless! she might have been burned to death," said Mary, lifting her hands. "She would have been much more burnt had it not been for her presence of mind," said Charles slowly. Miss Taylor laid down her knitting and approached the tea-table, none must preside at the meals but herself. She inquired of Charles whether he was going out again. "I think not," he replied indecisively, "I should like to have gone though, the doctor tells me Mary Ann Brewster is worse." "Weaker I conclude," said Mary. "Weaker than she has been at all, he thinks there is no hope for her now. No, I will not disturb them," he positively added, "it would be nearly twelve by the time I reached there."

# III

## Charles Taylor Receives a Message

W hat a loud ring," exclaimed Mary Taylor, as the bell, pulled with no gentle hand, echoed and echoed through the house; "should it be cousin George come home, he thinks he will let us know who is there." It was not George. A servant entered the room with a telegram, "the man is waiting, sir," he said, holding out the paper for Charles to sign. Charles affixed his signature and took up the dispatch; it came from Waterville, Mary laid her hand upon it ere it was open, her face looked ghastly pale. "A moment of preparation," she said. "Now, Mary, do not anticipate evil, it may not be ill news at all." He glanced his eye rapidly and privately over it while Martha came and stood near with a stifled sob, then he held it out to Mary, reading it aloud at the same time, "Mrs. Bangs to Charles Taylor, come at once to Waterville, Mr. Bangs wishes to see you." Mary, her extreme fears having been relieved, took refuge in displeasure. "What does Mrs. Bangs mean by sending a vague message like that?" she uttered. "Is Mr. Bangs worse, is he sick, is he in danger or has the summons not reference at all to his state of health?" Charles had taken it in his hand again and was studying the words—as we are all apt to do when in uncertainty.

He could make no more out of them. "Mrs. Bangs might have been more explicit," he resumed. "She has no right to play upon our fears," said Mary. "Well, what are you going to do?" inquired Mary of her brother. "I will do as the dispatch desires me, go at once, which will be at midnight." "Give it to me again," said Mary. He put the dispatch into her hand, and she sat down with it, apparently studying its every word. "Vague! Vague! Can anything be possibly more vague," she exclaimed. "It leaves us utterly in doubt of her motive for sending, she must have done it on purpose to try our feelings." "She has done it in carelessness, carelessness," surmised Charles. "Which is as reprehensible as the other," severely answered Mary. "Charles, when you get there, should you find him dangerously ill dispatch to us at once." "I should be sure to do so," was his answer. "Where are you going?" asked Mary, for he was preparing to go out. "As far as Mrs. Brewster's." Leaving the warm room for the street, the night air seemed to strike upon him with a chill which he had not experienced when he went out previously, and he returned and put on his overcoat. He could not leave before 2 o'clock, unless he had engaged a special train, which the circumstances did not appear to call for. At 2 o'clock a mail train passed through the place, stopping at all stations, and on that he concluded to go. He walked briskly along the path, his thoughts running upon many things, but chiefly on the unsatisfactory dispatch, very unsatisfactory he felt it to be, and a vague fear crossed his mind that his friend and partner might be in danger, looking at it from a sober point of view his judgment said "no," but we cannot always look at suspense soberly, neither could Charles Taylor.

Before reaching Madam Brewster's on the walk that Charles had taken, you pass the church and residence of Parson Davis. Nature had not intended Mr. Davis for a pastor, and his sermons were the bane of his life; an excellent man, a most efficient pastor for a village, a gentleman, a scholar, abounding in good, practical sense, but not a preacher; sometimes he wrote sermons, sometimes he tried them without the book, but let him do as he would, there was always a conviction of failure as to his sermons winning their way to his hearers hearts. He was of medium height, keen features, black hair, mingled with gray. The house was built of white stone and was a commodious residence; some of the rooms had been added to the house of late years. Mrs. Davis' room was very pleasant to sit in on a summer's day when the grass was green and the many colored flowers with their gay brightness and their perfume gladdened the senses, and the birds were singing and the bees and butterflies sporting. Mrs. Davis was a lady-like woman of middle height and fair complexion, she was remarkably susceptible to surrounding influences, seasons and weather held much power over her. A dark figure was leaning over the gate of Parson Davis, shaded by the dark trees, but though the features of the face were obscure, the outline of the clerical hat was visible, and by that Mr. Davis was known. Charles Taylor stopped: "You are going this way late" said the parson. "It is late for a visit to Mrs. Brewster's, but I wish particularly to see them." "I have just returned from there," said Mr. Davis. "Mary Ann grows weaker, I hear." "Yes, I have been holding prayer with her." Charles Taylor felt shocked. "Is she so near death as that," he inquired in a hushed tone. "So near death as that" repeated Mr. Davis in an accent of reproof. "I did not expect to hear such a remark from you, Mr. Taylor; my friend, is it only when death is near that we are to pray?" "It is mostly when death is near that prayers are held over us," replied Charles Taylor. "True, for those who have known when and how to pray for themselves; look at that girl passing away from among us, with all her worldly thoughts, her selfish habits, her evil, peevish temper, but God's ways are not like our ways; we might be tempted to ask why such as these are removed, such as Janey left, the one child as near akin to an angel as it is possible to be here; the other, in our blind judgment, we may wonder that she, most ripe for heaven, should not be taken to it, and the other one left to be pruned and dug around, to have, in short, a chance given her of making herself better." "Is she so very sick?" "I think her so, as well as the doctor, it was what he said that sent me up; her frame of mind is not a desirable one, and I have been doing my best; I shall be with her again to-morrow." He continued his way and Mr. Davis looked after him until his form disappeared in the shadows cast by the roadside trees. The clock was striking twelve when Charles Taylor opened the iron gate that led to Mrs. Brewster's house; the house, with the exception of one window looked dark, even the hall lamp was out and he was afraid that all had retired. From that window a dull light shone behind the blind; a stationary light it had been of late, to be seen by any wayfarer all night long for it came from the sick girl's room. A rap upon the door brought Eliza.

"Oh, sir," she exclaimed in surprise of seeing him so late, "I think Miss Janey has gone to bed." Mrs. Brewster came running down the stairs as he stepped into the hall; she also was surprised at his late visit. "I would not have disturbed you, but I am about to depart for Waterville," he explained. "A telegram has arrived from Mrs. Bangs, calling me there. I should like to see Janey before I go. I don't know how long I may be gone." "I sent Janey to her bed, her head ached," said Mrs. Brewster, "she has not been up very long. Oh, Mr. Taylor, this has been such a day of grief, heads and and hearts alike aching." Charles Taylor entered the drawing-room, and Mrs. Brewster proceeded to her daughter's chamber; softly opening the door, she looked in. Janey, undisturbed by the noise of his visit, for she had not supposed it to be a visit relating to her, was kneeling down by the bed saying her prayers, her face buried in her hands, and the light from the candle shining on her smooth hair. A minute or so her mother remained silent, and then Janey arose; she had not begun to undress. It was the first intimation she had that anyone was there, and she recoiled with surprise. "Mamma, how you scared me! Mary Ann is not worse?" "She can't well be worse on this side of the grave. Mr. Taylor is in the drawing-room, and wishes to see you." She went down at once. Mrs. Brewster did not go with her, but went into her sick daughter's room. The fire in the drawing-room was low, and Eliza had been in to stir it up. Charles stood before it with Janey, telling her of his unexpected journey. The red embers threw a glow upon her face, her brow looked heavy, her eyes swollen. He saw the signs, and laid his hand fondly on her head. "What has given you the headache, Janey?" The tears came into her eyes. "It does ache very much," she answered. "Has crying caused it?" "Yes," she said, "it is of no use to deny it, for you could have seen it by my swollen eyelids. I have wept to-day until it seems I can weep no longer, and it has made my eyes ache and my heart dull and heavy." "But, my dear, you should not give way to this grief; it may render you seriously ill." "Oh, Charles, how can I help it," she replied with emotion, as the tears rolled swiftly down her cheeks.

"We begin to see that there is no hope of Mary Ann's recovery; the doctor told mamma so to-day, and he sent over Mr. Davis." "Will grieving alter it?" Janey wept silently; there was full and complete confidence between her and Charles Taylor. She could tell him all her thoughts, her troubles, as she could a mother if she had one that loved her. "If she was more ready to go, the pain would seem less," breathed Janey. "That is, we might feel more reconciled to losing her, but you know how she is, Charles, when I have tried to talk to her about Heaven, she would not listen. She said it made her dull; it gave her the horrors. How can she, who has never thought of God, be fit to meet him?" Janey's tears were deepening into sobs. Charles Taylor thought of what the minister had said to him. His hand still rested on the head of Janey. "You are fit to meet him," he exclaimed, sadly. "Janey, what makes such a difference between you, you are sisters, raised in the same home?" "I do not know," said Janey, slowly, "I have always thought a great deal about Heaven ever since I first went to Sunday-school." "And why not Mary Ann?" "She would not go; she liked balls, parties and such like." Charles smiled; the words were so simple and natural. "Had the summons gone forth for you instead of her, it would have brought you no dismay?" "Only that I must leave all of my friends behind me," she answered, looking up at him, a bright smile shining through her tears. "I should know that God would not take me unless it was for the best. Oh, Charles, if we could only save her!" "Child, you contradict yourself. If what God does must be for the best, you should reconcile yourself to parting with Mary Ann." "Yes," hesitated Janey, "but I fear she has never thought of it herself or in any way prepared for it." "Do you know that I am going to find fault with you, Janey?" he added, after a pause. She turned her eyes upon him in complete surprise, the tears drying up. "Did you not promise me—did you not promise the doctor that you would not enter your sister's chamber while the fever was upon her?" The hot color flashed into her face. "Forgive me, Charles," she whispered, "I could not help myself; Mary Ann, on the fifth morning of her illness, began to cry for me very much, and mamma came to my room and asked me to go to her. I told her that the doctor had forbidden me and that I had promised you; it made her angry; she took me by the arm and pulled me in." Charles stood looking at her; there was nothing to answer. He had known in his deep and trusting love that it was no fault of Janey's. Thinking he was vexed, she answered, "You know, Charles, so long as I am here in mamma's home, her child, it is to her that I owe obedience; as soon as I am your wife I shall owe it and give it to you." "You are right, my darling." "And it has been productive of no ill consequences," she said. "I did not catch the fever; had I found myself growing the least sick, I should have sent for you and told you all." "Janey," he cried, "had you caught the fever I should never have forgiven those who led you into the danger."

"Listen," said Janey, "mamma is calling." Mrs. Brewster had been calling to Mr. Taylor. Thinking that she was not heard she came down the stairs and entered the room wringing her hands; her eyes were moist, her sharp thin red nose was redder then ever. "Oh, dear, I don't know what I shall do with her," she sobbed. "She is so sick and fretful, Mr. Taylor, nothing will satisfy her now but she must see you." "See me," repeated he. "She will," she says. "I told her you was leaving for Waterville and she burst out crying and said if she was to die she would never see you again, do you mind going in, you are not afraid?" "No, I am not afraid," said Charles, "the infection can not have remained all this while, and if it had I should not fear it." Mrs. Brewster led the way upstairs, Charles followed her, Janey came in afterwards. Mary Ann lay in bed, her thin face, drawn and white, raised upon the pillow, her hollow eyes were strained forward with a fixed look. Sick as he had thought her to have been he was hardly prepared to see her like this; and it shocked him. "Why have you never come to see me?" she asked in a hollow voice as he approached and leaned over her, "you would never have come till I died, you only care for Janey." "I would have come to see you had I known you wished it," he answered, "but you do not look strong enough to receive visitors." "They might cure me if they would," she said, her breath panting, "I want to go away somewhere and that Brown won't let me; if it were Janey he would cure her." "He will let you go as soon as you are able," said Charles. "Why did this fever come to me, why didn't it go to Janey instead, she is strong and would have got well in no time, that is not fair." "My dear child you must not excite yourself," implored her mother. "I will speak," cried Mary Ann with a touch, feeble though it was, of her peevish vehemence. "Nobody's thought of but Janey, if you had your way," looking hard at Mr. Taylor, "she would not have been allowed to come near me, no, not if I had died." She altered into whimpering tears, her mother whispered to him to leave the room, it would not do, this excitement. "I will come and see you again when you are better," he soothingly whispered. "No, you won't," said Mary Ann, "and I shall be dead when you return, good-by, Charles Taylor." These last words were called after him as he left the room, her mother went with him to the door, her eyes full, "you see there is no hope of her," she wailed. Charles did not think there was, it appeared to him that in a few hours, hope for Mary Ann would be over. Janey waited for him in the hall and was leading the way to the drawing-room, but he told her that he could not stay longer and opened the door. "I wish you were not going away," she said, her spirits being very unequal caused her to see things with a gloomy eye. "I wish you were going with me," said he, "don't cry, I shall soon be back again." "Everything makes me cry to-night, you might not get back until the worst is over, oh, if she could be saved." He held her face close to him and took from it his farewell kiss. "God bless you, my darling, forever." "May he bless you Charles," she said, with streaming eyes and for the first time in her life his kiss was returned, then they parted.

# IV

## An Unexpected Death

Charles having reached the station, taken the train to Waterville in response to the telegram, and when he reached there taken a carriage and was driven to the residence of Marshall Bangs, he found the decaying invalid sitting on a sofa in his bed-room; he had just recovered from a fainting spell, and he had recovered only to be the more weak. He was standing on the lawn before his house talking with a friend when he suddenly fell to the ground. He did not recover consciousness until evening, and nearly the first wish he expressed was a desire to see his friend and partner, Charles Taylor. "Dispatch for him" he said to his wife. Mrs. Bangs had a horror for fevers, especially when they were confined to everybody; at the present time she considered herself out of the reach of it, and no amount of persuasion could induce her to return, but her husband had grown tired and restless and was determined to go home, but let her remain until the fever had taken its departure, hence the dispatch. On the second day he was well enough to converse with Charles on business affairs, and that over, he expressed the wish that Charles would take him home. Charles mentioned it to Mrs. Bangs; it did not meet her approbation. "You should have opposed it entirely," she said, in a firm tone. "But why so, Mrs. Bangs, if he desires to return, I think he should." "Not while the fever lingers there; were he to take it and die I should never forgive myself." Charles had no fear of the fever for himself, and did not fear it for his friend; he intimated as much, "it is not the fever that will hurt him, Mrs. Bangs." "You have no right to say that. Mrs. Brewster, a month ago, would have said that she did not fear it for Mary Ann, and now she is dying, or dead, you confess you did not think that she could last more than a day or two when you left." "I certainly did not," said Charles. "She looked fearfully ill and emaciated, but that has nothing to do with Mr. Bangs." "I cannot conceive how you could be so imprudent as to venture into her sick-room," cried Mrs. Bangs, "indeed that you went to the house at all while the fever was in it." "There could be no risk in my going into her room, nothing is the matter with her now but debility." "We cannot tell, Mr. Taylor, when risk ends or when it begins; had not so many hours elapsed before you came here I should feel afraid of you." Charles smiled. But he wished he had said nothing of his visit to the sick-room, for he was one of those who observe strict consideration for the feelings and prejudices of others; there was no help for it now. "It is not I that shall be returning to Bellville yet," said Mrs. Bangs, "the sickly old place must give proof of its renewed health first; you will not get either me nor Mr. Bangs there for quite a while."

"What does the doctor think of the fever, that it will linger long?" "On the night I came away he told me he believed it was going at last. I hope he will prove right."

Charles Taylor spoke to his partner of his marriage arrangements. He had received a letter from Mary the morning after he left, in which she agreed to the proposal that Janey should be her temporary guest. This removed all barriers to the immediate union. "But, Charles, suppose Mary Ann should die," observed Mr. Bangs. This conversation was taking place on the day previous to their leaving Waterville, where Charles had now been three days. "In that case, I suppose it will have to be postponed," he replied, "but I hope for better news. That she is not dead yet is certain, or they would have written to me, and in such cases, if a patient can pull through the first debility, recovery may be possible." "Have you heard from Janey?" "No. I have written to her twice, but in each letter I told her I would soon be home; therefore, most likely she did not write, thinking it would miss me. Had the worst happened, they would have written to me at all events." "So you will marry soon, if she lives?" "Very soon." "I hope that God will bless you both," cried the invalid. "She will be a wife in a thousand." Charles thought she would, but did not say so. "I wish I had never left Bellville," he said, turning his haggard, but still fine blue eyes upon his friend. Charles was silent. None had regretted the departure more than he. "I wish I could go back to it to die." "My dear friend, I hope you may live many years to bless us. If you can get through the winter, and I see no reason why you should not, with care, you may regain your strength and be as well as ever." The invalid shook his head. "It will never be." While they were thus engaged a servant called Charles from the room. A telegram had arrived for him at the station, and a boy had brought it over. A conviction of what it contained flashed over Charles Taylor's heart as he opened it; the death of Mary Ann Brewster. From Mrs. Brewster it proved to be, not much more satisfactory than Mrs. Bangs, for if hers was unexplanatory this was incoherent. "The breath has just left my daughter's body. Mrs. Brewster." Charles returned to the room, his mind full; in the midst of his sorrow and regret for Mary Ann, his compassion for her mother, and he did really feel sorry, intruded the thoughts of his marriage; it must be postponed now. "What did he want with you," asked Mr. Bangs when Charles returned to him. "He brought me a telegram from Bellville." "A business message?" "No, sir; from Mrs. Brewster." By the tone of his voice, by the falling of his countenance, he could read what had occurred, but he kept silent, waiting for him to speak. "Poor Mary Ann is gone." "It will make a delay in your plans, Charles," said Mr. Bangs sorrowfully, after some minutes had been given to expressions of regret. "It will, sir." The invalid leaned back in his chair, and said in a low voice, "I shall not be long after her, I feel that I shall not."

Very early indeed did they start in the morning, long before daybreak. They would reach Bellville at twelve at night, all things being well; a weary day, a long one at any rate, and the train steamed into Bellville. The clock was striking twelve. Mr. Bangs' carriage stood waiting. A few minutes was spent in collecting baggage. "Shall I give you a seat as far as the bank, Mr. Taylor?" inquired Mr. Bangs. "Thank you; no I shall just go for a minute's call on Mrs. Brewster." Mr. Davis who was in the station getting mail heard the words, he turned hastily, caught Charles by the hand and drew him aside. "Are you aware of what has happened?" "Yes," replied Charles, "Mrs. Brewster telegraphed to me last night." Mr. Davis pressed his hand and moved on, Charles taking the road that would lead him to Mrs. Brewster's house. It is now ten days since he was there, the house looked precisely as it did then, all in darkness, except the dull light that burned from Mary Ann's sick room; it burnt there still; then it was lighting the living; now—Charles Taylor rang the bell gently, does any one like to go with a fierce peal to a house where death is an inmate? Eliza opened the door as usual and burst into tears when she saw who it was. "I said it would bring you back, sir!" she exclaimed. "Does Mrs. Brewster bear it pretty well," he asked, as she showed him into the drawing-room. "No, sir; not over well," sobbed the girl. "I'll tell the mistress that you are here." He stood over the fire as he had done before, it was low now like it was then, strangely still seemed the house, he could almost have told that one was lying dead in it, he listened waiting for the step of Janey, hoping that she would be the first to meet him. Eliza returned. "My mistress says, would you be kind enough to come to her." Charles followed her upstairs, she went to the room where he had been taken the other time, Mary Ann's room, in reality the room of Mrs. Brewster; but it had been given to Mary Ann for her sickness. Eliza with soft tread crossed the corridor to the door and opened it. Was she going to show him into the presence of the dead. He thought she must have mistaken Mrs. Brewster's orders and he hesitated on the threshhold. "Where is Miss Janey," he whispered. "Who, sir;" "Miss Janey, is she well?" The girl stared at him, flung the door wide open and gave a loud cry as she flew down the stairs. He looked after her in amazement, had she gone mad, then he turned and walked into the room with a hesitating step. Mrs. Brewster was coming forward to meet him, she was convulsed with grief, he took both her hands in his with a soothing gesture, essaying a word of comfort, not of inquiry why she should have brought him to this room, he glanced at the bed expecting to see the corpse upon it; but the bed was empty and at that moment his eyes caught another sight.

Seated by the fire in an invalid chair surrounded by pillows covered with shawls, with a wan, attenuated face and eyes that seemed to have a glaze over them was—who? Mary Ann? It certainly was Mary Ann, in life yet, for she feebly held out her hand in welcome, and the tears suddenly gushed from her eyes, "I am getting better, Mr. Taylor." Charles Taylor—how shall I write it, for one minute he was blind to what it could all mean, his whole mind was a chaos of astonished perplexity, and then when the dreadful truth burst upon him he staggered against the wall with a wailing cry of agony, it was Janey who had died. Charles Taylor leaned against the wall in his shock of agony; it was one of those moments that can come only once in a life-time, in many lives never, when the greatest of earthly misery bursts upon the startled spirit, shattering it for all time. Were Charles Taylor to live a hundred years he could never know another moment like this, the power so to feel would have left him. It had not left him yet; it had scarcely come to him in its full realization; at present he was half stunned. Strange as it may seem, the first impression upon his mind was that he was so much nearer the next world. How am I to define this nearness? It was not that he was nearer to it by time or in goodness; nothing of that.

# V

## CHARLES TAYLOR'S REGRETS

Janey had passed within its portals, and the great gulf which divides time from eternity seemed to be but a span. Now, to Charles Taylor, it was as if he in spirit had followed her in from being a place far off. Vague, indefinite, indistinct, it had suddenly been brought to him close and palpable, or he to it. Had Charles Taylor been an atheist, denying a hereafter—Heaven in its compassion have mercy upon all such—that one moment of suffering would have recalled him to a sense of his mistake. It was as if he looked aloft with the eyes of inspiration and saw the truth; it was as a brief passing moment of revelation from God. She, with her loving spirit, her gentle heart, her simple trust in God, had been taken from this world to enter upon a better. She was as surely living in it, had entered upon its mysteries, its joys, its rest as that he was living here. She, he believed, was as surely regarding him now, and his great sorrow as that he was left alone to battle with it. From this time Charles Taylor possessed a lively, ever-present link with that world, and knew that its gates would, in God's good time, be open for him. These feelings, impressions, facts—you may designate them as you please—took up their places in his mind, all in that first instant, and seated themselves there forever; not yet very consciously to his stunned senses. In his weight of bitter grief nothing could be to him very clear; ideas passed through his brain quickly, confusedly, like unto the changing scenes in a phantasmagoria. He looked round as one bewildered, the bed smoothed ready for occupancy, on which on entering he had expected to see the dead, but not her. There was between him and the door Mary Ann Brewster, in her invalid chair by the fire, a table at her right hand, covered with adjuncts of the sick room, a medicine bottle with its accompanying wine-glass and tablespoon, jelly and other delicacies to tempt a faded appetite.

Mary Ann sat there and gazed at him with her hollow eyes, from which the tears dropped slowly on her cadaverous cheeks. Mrs. Brewster stood before him, sobs choking her voice, wringing her hands. Yes, both were weeping, but he—It is not in the presence of others that man gives way to grief, neither will tears come to him in the first leaden weight of anguish. Charles Taylor listened mechanically, as one cannot do otherwise, to the explanations of Mrs. Brewster. "Why did you not prepare me? why did you let it come upon me with this startling shock?" was his first remonstrance. "I did prepare you," sobbed Mrs. Brewster. "I telegraphed to you as soon as it happened; I wrote the message to you with my own hand, and sent it to the office before I turned my attention to anything else." "I received the message, but you did not say—I thought it was—" Charles Taylor turned his eyes toward Mary Ann. He remembered her condition in the midst of his own anguish and would not alarm her. "You did not mention Janey's name," he continued, to Mrs. Brewster; "how could I suppose you alluded to her or that she was sick?" Mary Ann divined his motive of hesitation; she was uncommonly keen in penetration, sharp—as the world goes—as the world says, and she had noted his words on entering, when he began to soothe Mrs. Brewster for the loss of a child. She had noticed his startled recoil when the news fell on him. She spoke up; a touch of her old vehemence; the tears stopped on her face and her eyes glistened. "You thought it was I who had died! Yes, you did, Mr. Taylor; and you need not try to deny it; you would not have cared, so that it was not Janey." Charles had no intention of contradicting her; he turned from her in silence to look inquiringly and reproachfully at her mother. "Mr. Taylor, I could not prepare you better than I did," said Mrs. Brewster, "when I wrote the letter telling of her illness." "What letter?" interrupted Charles; "I received no letter." "But you must have received it," replied Mrs. Brewster, in her quick and sharp manner, not sharp with him, but from a rising doubt whether the letter had been miscarried. "I wrote it, and I know that it was safely mailed; you should have received it before you did the dispatch." "I never had it," said Charles. "When I waited in your drawing-room now I was listening for Janey's footsteps to come to me." Charles Taylor upon inquiry found that the letter had arrived duly and safely at Waterville at the time mentioned by Mrs. Brewster, but it appears that it was overlooked by the postmaster; but the shock had come now. He took a seat by the table, and covered his eyes with his hands, as the mother gave him a detailed account of her sickness and death. Not all the account that she or anybody else could give could take one iota from the dreadful fact staring him in the face; she was gone, gone forever from this world; he could never meet the glance of her eyes again or hear her voice in response to his own. Ah! reader, there are griefs that tell, rending the heart as an earthquake would rend the

SARAH E. FARRO

earth, and all that can be done is to sit down under them and ask of heaven strength to bear—to bear as best we can, until time shall shed a few drops of healing balm from its wings.

On the last night that Charles had seen her, Janey's eyes and brow were heavy, she had cried much during the day and supposed the pain to have arisen from that circumstance. She had given this explanation to Charles Taylor. Neither he nor she had a thought that it could come from any other source. More than a month ago Mary Ann had taken the fever; fears of it for Janey had passed away, and yet those dull eyes, that hot head, that heavy weight of pain, were only the symptoms of the sickness approaching. A night of tossing and turning, in fits of disturbed sleep, of terrifying dreams, and Janey awoke to the conviction that the fever was upon her.

About the time she generally arose she rang the bell for Eliza. "I do not feel well," she said, "as soon as mamma is up will you ask her to come to me? do not disturb her before."

Eliza obeyed her orders. But her mother, tired and worn out with her attendance upon Mary Ann, with whom she had been up half the night, did not rise until between nine and ten. The maid went to her then and delivered the message.

"In bed, still; Miss Janey in bed, still?" exclaimed Mrs. Brewster. She spoke in much anger, for Janey had to be up in time, attending to Mary Ann, it was required of her to be so. Throwing on a dressing-gown, Mrs. Brewster proceeded to Janey's room, and there she broke into a storm of reproach and anger, never waiting to ascertain what might be the matter with Janey, anything or nothing.

"Ten o'clock, and that poor child to have been till now with nobody to go near her but a servant!" she reiterated, "you have no feeling, Janey!"

Janey drew the covering from her flushed face and turned her glittering eyes, dull last night, shining with the fever now upon her, upon her mother.

"Oh, mamma, I am sick; indeed I am. I can hardly lift my head for the pain; feel how hot it is. I did not think I ought to get up."

"What is the matter with you?" sharply inquired Mrs. Brewster.

"I cannot tell," answered Janey, "I know that I feel sick all over. I feel, mamma, as if I could not get up."

"Very well; there's that dear, suffering angel lying alone, and you can think of yourself before her; if you choose to lie in bed you must, but you will reproach yourself for your selfishness when she is gone; another twenty-four hours and she may not be with us; do as you think best."

Janey burst into tears and caught hold of her mother's robe as she was turning away. "Mamma, do not be angry with me; I hope I am not selfish, mamma," and her voice sank to a whisper, "I have been thinking that it may be the fever."

"The fever?" reproachfully echoed Mrs. Brewster, "Heaven help you for a selfish and fanciful child; did I not send you to bed with a headache last night, and what is it but the remains of that headache that you feel this morning? I can see what it is, you have been fretting about the departure of Charles Taylor; get up out of that hot bed and dress yourself, and come in and attend on your sister; you know she can't bear to be waited on by anybody but you; get up, I say."

Will Mrs. Brewster remember this to her dying day? I should were I in her place. She suppressed all mention of it to Charles Taylor. "The dear child told me that she did not feel well, but I only thought she had the headache and that she would feel better up," were the words that she used to him.

What sort of a vulture was gnawing at her heart as she spoke them? It was true that in her blind selfishness for one undeserving child she had lost sight of the fact that sickness could come to Janey; she had not allowed herself to believe the probability; she, who accused of selfishness that devoted, generous girl, who was ready at all hours to put her hands under her sister's feet, and would have given her own life to save Mary Ann's. Janey got up, got up as best she could, her limbs aching, her head burning; she went into her sister's room and did for her what she was able, gently, lovingly, anxiously, as before. Ah, my dear reader, let us be thankful that it was so; it is well to be stricken down in the active path of duty, working until we can work no more. She did so. She stayed where she was until the day was half gone, bearing up it is hard to say how. She could not eat breakfast; she could not eat anything. None saw how sick she was; her mother was wilfully blind. Mary Ann had eyes and thoughts for herself alone. "What are you shivering for?" her sister once fretfully asked her. "I feel cold, dear," was Janey's unselfish answer; not a word more did she say of her illness. In the afternoon Mrs. Brewster was away from the room attending to domestic affairs, and when she returned the doctor was there; he had been prevented from calling earlier in the day; they found Mary Ann dropped into a doze and Janey stretched out on the floor before the fire, groaning; but the groans ceased as she entered. The doctor, regardless of the waking invalid, strode up to Janey and turned her face to the light. "How long has she been like this?" he asked, his voice shrill with emotion. "Child, child, why did they not send for me?" Poor Janey was then too sick to reply. The doctor carried her up to her room in his arms, and the servants undressed her and laid her in the bed from which she was never more to rise. The fever took violent hold of her, precisely as it had attacked Mary Ann, though scarcely as bad, and danger for Janey was not looked for by her mother. Had Mary Ann not got over a similar crisis they would have feared for Janey, so given are we to judge by collateral circumstances. It was on the fourth or fifth day that highly dangerous symptoms supervened, and then her mother wrote to Charles the letter which had not reached him; there was this much of negative consolation to be derived from the non-receipt, that had it been delivered to him on the instant of its arrival he could not have been in time to see her. "You ought to have written to me as soon as she was taken sick," he said to Mrs. Brewster. "I would have done it had I apprehended danger," she repentantly answered, "but I never did, and the doctor never did. I thought how pleasant it would be to get her safely through the danger and sickness before you knew of it." "Did she not wish me written to?" The question was asked firmly, abruptly, after the manner of one who will not be cheated out of his answer. Her mother could not evade it; how could she, with her child lying dead over her head?

"It is true she did wish it, it was on the first day of her illness that she spoke, 'Write and tell Charles Taylor,' she never said it but once." "And you did not," he uttered, his voice hoarse with emotion. "Do not reproach me! Do not reproach me!" cried Mrs. Brewster, clasping her hands in supplication, and the tears falling in showers from her eyes, "I did all for the best, I never supposed there was danger. I thought what a pity it would be to bring you back such a long journey, putting you to so much unnecessary trouble and expense." Trouble and expense—in a case like that she could speak of expense to Charles—but he thought how she had to battle with both trouble and expense her whole life long, and that for her they must wear a formidable aspect, he remained silent. "I wish now I had written," she resumed in the midst of her choking sobs, "as soon as the doctors said there was danger, I wished it, but," as if she would seek to excuse herself, "what with the two upon my hands, she upstairs, Mary down here, I had not a moment for proper reflection." "Did you tell her you had not written?" he asked, "or did you let her lie day after day, hour after hour, waiting and blaming me for my careless neglect?" "She never blamed any one, you know she did not," wailed Mrs. Brewster, "and I think she was too sick to think even of you, she was only sensible at times. Oh, I say, do not reproach me, Mr. Taylor, I would give my own life to bring her back. I never knew her worth until she was gone, I never loved her as I love her now." There could be no doubt that Mrs. Brewster was reproaching herself far more bitterly than any reproach could tell upon her from Charles Taylor, an accusing conscience is the worst of all evils. She sat there, her head bent, swaying herself backwards and forwards on her chair, moaning and crying. It was not a time Charles felt to say a word of her past heartless conduct in forcing Janey to breathe the infection of her sister's sick room, and all that he could say, all the reproaches, all the remorse and repentance would not bring her back to life. "Would you like to see her," whispered her mother, as he rose to go? "Yes." She lighted a candle and led the way upstairs. Janey had died in her own room. At the door he took the candle from Mrs. Brewster. "I must go in alone." He passed into the chamber and closed the door, on the bed laid out in a white robe, lay all that remained of Janey Brewster. Pale, still, pure, her face was wonderfully like what it had been in life, and a calm smile rested upon it, but Charles wished to be alone. Mrs. Brewster stood outside, leaning against the opposite wall, weeping silently, the glimmer from the hall lamp below faintly lighting the corridor, and she fancied that a sound of choking struck upon her ears, and she pulled around her a small black shawl that she wore, for grief had made her chilly, and wept the faster. He came out by and by, calm and quiet as ever, he did not see Mrs. Brewster standing there in the dimly lighted hall, and went straight down, carrying the candle. Mrs. Brewster caught up with him at Mary Ann's room, and took the candle from him.

"She looks very peaceful, does she not?" was her whisper. "She could not look otherwise." He went on down alone, intending to let himself out, but Eliza had heard his steps and was waiting at the door. "Good night Eliza," he said, as he passed her. The girl did not answer, she slipped out into the yard after him. "Oh, sir, and didn't you hear of it?" she whispered. "No." "If anybody was ever gone away to be an angel, sir, its that sweet young lady, sir," said Eliza, letting her tears and sobs come forth as they would, "She was just one here and she has gone to her own fit place." "Yes, that is so." "You should have been in this house throughout the whole of the illness to have seen the difference between them, sir. Nobody would believe it; Miss Brewster angry and snappish, and not caring who suffered or who was sick, or who toiled, so that she was served, Miss Janey lying like a tender lamb, patient and meek, thankful for all that was done for her. It does seem hard, sir, that we should lose her forever." "Not forever, Eliza," he answered. "And that is true, too; but sir, the worst is, one can't think of that sort of consolation just when one's troubles are the freshest. Good night, to you, sir." Charles Taylor walked on, leaving the high road for a less frequented one; he went along, musing in the depth of his great grief; there was no repining. He was one to trace the finger of God in all things. A more entire trust in God it was, perhaps, impossible for any one to feel than was felt by Charles Taylor; it was what he lived under. He could not see why Janey should have been taken, why this great sorrow should fall upon him, but that it must be for the best he implicitly believed— the best, for God had done it. How he was to live on without her he did not know. How he could support the lively anguish of the future he did not care to think. All his hopes in this life gone, all his plans, his projects uprooted by a single blow, never to return. He might look yet for the bliss of a Hereafter that remains for the most heavy laden, thank God, but his sun of happiness in this world had set forever. The moon was not shining as it was the night he left Janey, when he left his farewell kiss. Oh! that he could have known that it was the last on the gentle lips of Janey. There was no moon now; the stars were not showing themselves, for a black cloud enveloped the skies like a pall, fit accompaniment to his blasted hopes and his path altogether was dark. But, as he neared the office of the doctor, he could see him sitting in his accustomed place. Charles thought that he would like to have a few minutes conversation with him. He walked to the door, opened it, and saw that the doctor was alone.

# VI

## Dr. Brown Explains to Charles

Doctor, why did you not write to me?" the doctor brought down his fist on his desk with such force as to cause some of his vials to fall over and waste their contents; he had been bottling up his anger for some time against Mrs. Brewster, and this was the first explosion. "Because I understood that she had done so. I was there when the poor child asked her to do it. I found her on the floor in Mary Ann's room; on the floor, if you will believe it, lying there because she could not hold her head up. Her mother had dragged her out of the bed that morning, sick as she was, and forced her to attend as usual upon Mary Ann. I got it all out of Eliza. 'Mamma,' she said, when I pronounced it to be the fever, though she was almost beyond speaking then, 'you will write to Charles Taylor?' I never thought but what she had done it; your sister inquired if you had been written for and I told her yes." "Doctor," came the next sad words, "could you not have saved her?" The doctor shook his head and answered in a quiet tone, looking down at the stopper of a vial which he had caused to drop upon the floor, "neither care nor skill could save her. I did the best that could be done, Taylor," raising his quick, dark eyes, flashing them with a peculiar light; "she was ready to go; let it be your consolation." Charles Taylor made no answer, and there was a pause of silence. The doctor continued: "As to her mother, I hope that she may have her heart wrung with remembrance for years to come. I don't care what people preach about charity and forgiveness, I do wish it; but she will be brought to her senses, unless I am mistaken. She has lost her treasure and kept her bane a year or two more, and that is what Mary Ann will be." "She ought to have written to me." "She ought to do many things that she does not; she ought to have sent Janey from the house, as I told her, as soon as the disorder appeared in it. No, she kept her in her insane selfishness, and now I hope she is satisfied with her work. When alarming symptoms showed themselves in Janey, on the fourth day of her illness, I think it was, I said to her mother, it is strange what can be keeping Mr. Taylor. 'Oh,' said she, 'I did not write for him.' 'Not write!' I answered; and I fear I used an ugly word to her face. 'I'll write at once,' returned she, humbly. 'Of course,' said I, 'after the horse is stolen we always shut the barn door it's the way of the world.'" Another pause.

"I would have given anything to have taken Janey from the house at the time; to take her away from the town," observed Charles in a low tone. "I said so then, but it could not be." "I should have done it in your place," said the doctor; "if her mother had said no, I would have carried her away in front of her face. 'Not married,' you say. Rubbish to that; everybody knows she would have been safe with you, and you would have been married as soon as you could. What are forms and ceremonies and long tongues in comparison with a life like Janey's?" Charles Taylor leaned his head upon his hand, lost in the retrospect. Oh that he had taken her, that he had set at naught what he had then bowed to, the conventionalities of society, she might have been by his side now in health and life to bless him. Doubting words interrupted the train of thoughts. "And yet I don't know," the doctor was repeating in a dreamy manner, "what is to be will be; we look back, all of us, and say, if I had acted thus, if I had done the other thing, it would not have happened; events would have turned out differently, but who is to be sure of it. Had you carried Janey out of harm's way, as we might have thought, there is no telling but what she might have had the fever just the same; her blood might have become tainted before she left the house, there is no knowing, Mr. Taylor." "True. Good evening, doctor." He turned suddenly and hastily to go out of the door, but the doctor caught him before he had crossed the threshhold, and touched his arm to detain him. They stood there in obscurity, their faces shaded in the dusky night. "She left you a parting word, Mr. Taylor, an hour before she died; she was calm and sensible, though extremely weak. Mrs. Brewster had gone to her favorite, and I was left alone with Janey. 'Has he not come yet?' she asked me, opening her eyes. 'My dear,' I said, 'he could not come, he was never written for,' for I knew she alluded to you, and was determined to tell her the truth, dying though she was. 'What shall I say to him for you?' I continued. She raised her hand to motion my face nearer hers, for her voice was growing faint. 'Tell him, with my dear love, not to grieve,' she whispered between her panting breath, 'tell him that I am but gone on before.' I think they were almost the last words that she spoke." Charles Taylor leaned against the post of the office entrance, and drank in the words; then he shook the doctor's hand and departed, hurrying along like one who shrank from observation, for he did not care just then to encounter the gaze of his fellow-men. Coming with a quick step up the same street on which the office is situated was the Reverend Mr. Davis. He stopped to address the doctor. "Was that Mr. Taylor?" "Yes; this is a blow for him." Mr. Davis' voice insensibly sank to a whisper. "My wife tells me that he did not know of Janey's death and sickness until he arrived here. He thought it was Mary Ann who died; he went to her mother's thinking so." "Mrs. Brewster is a fool," was the complimentary rejoinder of the doctor. "She is in some things," warmly assented the pastor. "The telegram she sent was so obscurely worded as to cause him to assume that it was Mary Ann." "Well, she is only heaping burdens on her conscience," rejoined the doctor in a philosophic tone, "she has lost Janey through want of care, as I firmly believe, in not keeping her out of the way of the infection, she prevented their last meeting through not writing to him, she—"

"He could not have saved her had he been here," interrupted Mr. Davis. "Nobody said he could; there would have been satisfaction in it for him though, and for her, too, poor child." Mr. Davis did not contest the point, he was so very practical a man that he saw little use in last interviews; unless they were made productive of actual good he was disposed to regard such as bordering on the sentimental. "I have been over to see Bangs," he remarked. "They sent to the house after me while I was after mail; the boy said he did not believe he would live through the night and wanted the parson. I had a great mind to send word back that if he was in want of a parson he should have seen him before." "He's as likely to live through this night as he has been any night for the last six months," said the doctor. "Not a day since then but what he has been as likely to die as not." "And never to awaken to a thought that it might be desirable to make ready for the journey until the twelfth hour," exclaimed the parson. "'When I have a convenient season I will call for thee.' If I have been to see him once I have been twenty times," asserted the pastor, "and never could get him to pray. He wilfully put off all thought of death until the twelfth hour and then sends for me or one of my brethren and expects one hour's devotion will ensure his entrance into heaven. I don't keep the keys." "Did Bangs send for you or did the family?" inquired the doctor. "He, I expect; he was dressed for the occasion." "Will he live long?" "It is uncertain; he may last for six months or a year and he may die next week; it will be sudden when it does come." The pastor walked away at a brisk rate. Mrs. Davis was out of the room talking with some late applicant when he arrived at home. Laying aside her wrap Mrs. Davis seated herself before the fire in a quiet merino dress, the blaze flickering on her face betrayed to the keen glance of the pastor that her eyelashes were wet. "Grieving about Janey, I suppose?" his tone a stern one. "Well," continued the pastor, "she is better off. The time may come, we none of us know what is before us, when some of us who are left may wish we had died, as she has; many a one battling for very existence with the world's carking cares wails out a vain wish that he had been taken early from the evil to come." "It must be dreadful for Charles Taylor," she resumed, looking straight into the fire and speaking as if in communion with herself more than her husband. "Charley Taylor must find another love." It was one of those phrases spoken in satire only, to which the pastor of this village was occasionally given. He saw so much to condemn in the world, things which grated harshly on his superior mind, that his speech had become imbued with a touch of gall, and he would often give utterance to cynical remarks not at the time called for. There came a day, not long afterwards, when the residents of Bellville gathered at the church to hear and see the last of Janey Brewster. As many came inside as could, for it was known to the public that nothing displeased their pastor so much as to have irreverent idlers standing around the church staring and gaping and whispering their comments while he was performing the service of the burial of the dead, and his wishes were generally respected.

The funeral now was inside the church. It had been in so long that some eager watchers, estimating time by their impatience, began to think it was never coming out, but a sudden movement in the church reassured them. Slowly, slowly, on it came, the Reverend Mr. Davis leading the way, the coffin next, then came her mother and a few other relatives, and Charles Taylor with a stranger by his side; nothing more, save the pall-bearers with white scarfs and the necessary attendants. It was a perfectly simple funeral, corresponding well with what the dead had been in her simple life. The sight of this stranger took the curious gazers by surprise. Who was he? A stout gentleman, past middle age, holding his head high, with gold spectacles. He proved to be a cousin of Mrs. Brewster. The grave had been dug in a line with others not far from the edge of the burying ground. On it came, crossing the broad churchyard path which wound round to the road, crossing over patches of grass, treading between mounds and graves. The clergyman took his place at the head, the mourners near him, the rest disposing themselves quietly around. "Man, that is born of woman, hath but a short time to live, and is full of misery. He cometh up and is cut down like a flower; he fleeth as it were a shadow, and never continueth in one place." The crowd held their breath and listened and looked at Charles Taylor. He stood there, his head bowed, his face still, the gentle wind stirring his thin dark hair. It was probably a wonder to him in afterlife how he had contrived in that closing hour to retain his calmness before the world. "The coffin is lowered at last," broke out a little boy who had been more curious to watch the movements of the men than the aspect of Charles Taylor. "Hush, sir," sharply rebuked his mother, and the minister's voice again stole over the silence. "For as much as it has pleased Almighty God of His great mercy to take unto himself the soul of our dear sister here departed, we, therefore, commit her body to the ground, earth to earth, ashes to ashes, dust to dust, in sure and certain hope of the resurrection to eternal life, through our Lord Jesus Christ, who shall change our vile bodies that they may be like unto His glorious body, according to the mighty working whereby He is able to subdue all things to himself." Every word came home to Charles Taylor's senses, every syllable vibrated upon his heart-strings; that sure and certain hope laid hold of his soul never again to leave it. It diffused its own holy peace and calm in his troubled mind, and never until that moment did he fully realize the worth, the truth of her legacy. "Tell him that I am but gone on before," a few years. God, now present with him alone, knew how few or how many, and Charles Taylor would have joined her in eternal life. But why did the minister come to a temporary pause? Because his eyes had fallen upon one then coming up from the entrance of the burying ground to take his place among the mourners, and who had evidently arrived in a hurry. He wore neither scarf nor hat-band, nothing but a full suit of plain black clothes. "Look, mamma," cried a little boy. It was George Taylor, the cousin of Charles Taylor. He stood quietly by the side of his cousin, his hat in his hand, his head bowed, his curly hair waiving in the breeze. It was all the work of an instant, and the minister continued: "I heard a voice from heaven saying unto me, write, from henceforth blessed are the dead which die in the Lord, even so, sayeth the spirit, for they rest from their labors," and so went on the service to the end. The passage having been cleared, several mourning carriages were in waiting. Charles Taylor come forth leaning on his cousin's arm, both of them still bare headed. They entered one, the friends and relatives filled the others, and soon several men were shovelling earth upon the coffin as fast as they could, sending it with a rattle on the bright plate which told who was moldering within, Janey Brewster, aged twenty-one years. "Charles," cried his cousin George, leaning forward and seizing his cousin's hand impulsively, as the carriage moved slowly on, "I should have been here in good time, but for a delay in the train."

"Where did you hear of it? I did not know where to write to you," calmly asked Charles. "I heard of it in Gray Town and I came up here at once; Charles, could they not save her?" A slight negative movement was all Charles Taylor's answer.

The time went on, several months had passed, positions changed and Bellville was itself again; the unusually lovely weather which had prevailed so far as it had gone had put it into Mrs. Brown's head to give an out-door entertainment, the doctor had suggested that the weather might change, that there was no dependence to be placed in it, but she would not change her plans if the worst came to the worst, at the last moment she said they must do the best they could with them inside. But the weather was not fickle, the day rose warm, calm and wonderfully bright, and by five in the afternoon, most of the gay revellers had gathered on the grounds. George Taylor, a cousin of Charles arrived, one of the first; he was making himself conspicuous among the many groups, or perhaps, it was they that made him so by gathering around him, when two figures in mourning came up behind him, one of whom spoke "How do you do, Mr. George Taylor," he turned, and careless and thoughtless and graceless, as he was reported to be, a shock of surprise not unmixed with indignation swept over his feelings, for there standing before him were Mrs. Brewster and Mary Ann. She—Mary Ann—looked like a shadow, still peevish, white, discontented; what brought them there, was it so they showed their regrets for the dead Janey, was it likely that Mary Ann should appear at a feast of gayety in her weak state, sickly, not yet recovered from the effects of the fever, not yet out of the first deep mourning for Janey. "How do you do, Mrs. Brewster," very gravely responded George. Mrs. Brewster may have discerned somewhat his feelings from the expression on his face, not that he intentionally suffered it to rise in reproof of her. George Taylor did not set himself up in judgment against his fellow-men. Mrs. Brewster drew him aside with her after he had shaken hands with Mary Ann. "I am sure it must look strange to you to see us both here, Mr. Taylor, but poor child, she continues so weak and poorly that I scarcely know what to do with her, she set her heart upon coming here ever since Mrs. Brown's invitation arrived; she has talked of nothing else, and I thought it would not do to cross her." "Is Mr. Taylor here?" "Oh no," replied George, with more haste than he need have spoken. "I thought he would not be, I remarked so to Mary Ann when she expressed a hope for seeing him, indeed I think it was that hope which chiefly urged her to come; what have we done to him, Mr. George, he scarcely ever comes near the house?" "I don't know anything about it," returned George; "I can see that my cousin feels his loss deeply, yet it may be that visits to your house remind him of Janey too forcibly." "Will he ever marry, do you think?" said Mrs. Brewster, lowering her voice to a confidential whisper.

"At present I should be inclined to say he never would," answered George, wondering what in the world it would matter to her and thinking she evinced little sorrow or consideration for the memory of Janey. "But time works surprising changes," he added. "And time may affect Mr. Taylor," Mrs. Brewster paused, "How do you think she looks, my poor child?" "Miserable" almost rose to the tip of George's tongue, "she does not look well," he said aloud. "And she does so regret her dear sister, she's grieving after her always," said Mrs. Brewster, putting her handkerchief to her eyes. I don't believe it, thought George to himself. "How did you like Graytown?" she resumed, passing with little ceremony to another topic. "I liked it very well; all places are pretty much alike to a bachelor, Mrs. Brewster." "Yes, so they are, you won't remain a bachelor very long," continued Mrs. Brewster with a smile of jocularity. "Not so very long I dare say," acknowledged George. "It is possible I may put my head in the noose some time in the next ten years." She would have detained him further, but George did not care to be detained, he went after more attractive companionship. Chance or accident led him to Miss Flint, a niece of Mrs. Brown. Miss Flint had all her attractions about her that day, her bright pink silk—for pink was a favorite color of hers—was often seen by the side of George Taylor, once they strayed to the borders of a river in a remote part of the village, several were gathered there, a row on the water had been proposed and a boat stood ready, a small boat, capable of holding very few persons, but of these George and Julia Flint made two; could George have foreseen what that simple little excursion was going to do for him, he would not have taken part in it; how is it no sign of warning comes over us at these times; how many a day's pleasure began as a jubilee, how many a voyage entered upon in hope ends but in death. Oh, if we could but lift the veil what mistakes might be avoided! George Taylor, strong and active, took the oars, and when they had rowed about to their hearts' content and George was nearly overdone from exertion, they thought that they would land for awhile on what is called Dark Point, a mossy spot green and tempting to the eye. In stepping ashore Miss Flint tripped and lost her balance, and would have been in the water, but for George who saved her, but could not save her parasol, an elegant one, for which Miss Flint had paid a round sum of money just the day before; she naturally shrieked, when it went plunge into the water, and George, in recovering it, nearly lost his balance, and went in after the parasol, nearly not quite; he got himself pretty wet, but he made light of it, and sat on the grass with the others. The party were all young, old people don't venture much in skiffs, but had any been there of mature age, they would have ordered him home to get a change of clothes, and a glass of brandy. By and by he began to feel chilly, it might have occurred to him that the intense perspiration he had been in had struck inwards, but it did not. In the evening he was dancing with the rest of them thinking no more of it, apparently having escaped all ill effects from the wetting.

# VII

## John Smith's Dinner Party

The drawing-rooms of John Smith's mansion were teeming with light, with noise, and with company; a dinner party had taken place that day, a gentleman's party. It was not often that he gave one, and when he did it was thoroughly well done. George Taylor did not give better dinners than Mr. Smith. The only promised guest who had failed in his attendance was Charles Taylor. Very rarely indeed did he accept of invitations to dinner. If there was one man in all the county to whom Mr. Smith seemed inclined to pay court, to treat with marked consideration and respect, that man was Charles Taylor; he nearly always declined—declined courteously, in a manner which could not afford the slightest evidence of offense; he was of quiet habits, not strong in health of late, and, though he had to give dinner parties himself and attend some of his cousins' for courtesy's sake, his friends nearly all were kind enough to excuse him frequenting theirs in return. This time Charles Taylor had yielded to Mr. Smith's pressing entreaties made in person and promised to be present, a promise which was not, as it proved to be, kept. All the rest of the guests had assembled and they were only waiting the appearance of Mr. Taylor to sit down when a hasty note arrived from Miss Taylor. "Mr. Taylor was taken sick while dressing, and was unable to attend." So they sat down without him. The dinner having been over most of the guests had gone to the drawing-room, which was radiant with light and noisy with the hum of many voices. A few had gone home, a few had taken cigars and were strolling outside the dining-room windows in the bright moonlight. Miss Taylor's note that her brother had been taken sick while dressing for the dinner was correct; he was dressing in his room when he was attacked by a sharp internal pain, he hastily sat down, a cry escaping his lips and drops of water gathering on his brow; alone he bore it, calling for no aid; in a few minutes the paroxysm had partially passed and he rang for his servant, who had for many years attended his father. "George, I am sick again," said Charles, quietly. "Will you ask Miss Taylor to write a line to Mr. Smith, saying that I am unable to attend." George cast a strangely yearning look on the pale suffering face of his master, he had been in these paroxysms of pain once or twice. "I wish you would have Mr. Brown called in, sir," he cried. "I think I shall, he may give me some ease, possibly; take my message to your mistress, George." The effect of the message was to bring Mary to his room, "taken sick, a sharp inward pain," she was repeating after George. "Charles, what kind of a pain is it, it seems to me that you have had the same before?" "Write a few words the first thing, will you, Mary; I do not like to keep them waiting for me." Mary was as punctilious as Charles, and as considerate as he was for the convenience of others, and she sat down and wrote the note, dispatching it at once by Billy, another of the servants; few could have sat apart and done it as calmly as Mary, considering that she had a great thumping at her heart, a fear which had never penetrated it until this moment. Their mother's sickness was similar to this, a sharp acute pain had occasionally attacked her, the symptom of the inward malady of which she had died. Was the same fatal malady attacking him? The doctors had expressed their fears then that it might be hereditary. In the hall, as Mary was going back to Charles' room, the note having been written, she met George, the sad apprehensive look in the old man's face struck her, she touched his arm and motioned him into another room. "What is it that is the matter with your master?" "I don't know," was the answer; but the words were spoken in a tone which caused Mary to think that the old man was awake to the same fears that she was. "Miss Mary, I am afraid to think what it may be." "Is he often sick like this?" "I know but of a time or two ma'am, but that's a time or two too many." Mary entered his room, Charles was leaning back in his chair, his face ghastly, apparently prostrate from the effects of the pain; if a momentary thought had crossed her mind, that he might have written the note himself, it left her; now things were coming into her mind one by one, how much time he had spent in his room of late; how seldom, comparatively speaking, he went to his office; how often he called for the carriage, when he did go, instead of walking; only this last Sunday he had not gone near the church all day long, her fears grew into certainties. She took a chair, drawing it near to Charles, not speaking of her fears, but asking him in an agreeable tone how he felt, and what had caused his illness. "Have you had this pain before?" she continued, "Several times," he answered, "but it has been worse to-night than I have previously felt it. Mary I fear it may be the warning of my call, I did not think that I would leave you so soon." Except that Mary's face turned nearly as pale as his and that her fingers entwined themselves together so tightly as to cause pain, there was no outward sign of the grief that laid hold of her heart. "Charles, what is the complaint you are fearing?" she asked after a pause, "The same that my mother had," he quietly answered, speaking the words that Mary would not speak. "It may not be so," gasped Mary. "True, but I think it is." "Why have you never spoken of this?" "Because, until to-night, I have doubted whether it was so or not; the suspicion that it might be so, certainly was upon me, but it amounted to no more than a suspicion; at times when I feel quite well I argue that I must be wrong."

"Have you consulted a doctor?" "I am going to do so now. I have just sent George after one." "It should have been done before, Charles." "Why, if it is as I suspect, Brown and all his brethren cannot save me." Mary clasped her hands upon her knee and sat with her head bowed. It seemed that the only one left on earth with whom she could sympathize was Charles, and now perhaps he was going. The others had their own pursuits and interests, but she and Charles seemed to stand together; with deep sorrow for him, the brother whom she dearly loved, came other considerations, impossible not to occur to a practical, foreseeing mind like Mary's. His elbow on the arm of his chair, and his head resting upon his hand, sat Charles, his mind in as deep a reverie as his sister's. Where was it straying? To the remembrance of Janey, to the day that he had stood over her grave when they were placing her in it, was the time come, or nearly come, to which he had from that time looked forward—the time of his joining her. Perhaps the fiat of death could have come to few who could meet it as serenely as Charles Taylor. It would hardly be right to say welcome it, but certain it was that the prospect was one of pleasure rather than pain to him; to one who had lived near to God on earth the anticipation can bring no great dismay. It brought none to Charles Taylor, but he was not done with earth and its cares yet. Matilda Taylor was away from home that week, she had gone to spend it with some friends at a distance. Martha was alone when Mary returned to the drawing-room, she had no suspicion of the sorrow that was overhanging the house. She had not seen Charles go to his office, and felt surprised at his tardiness. "How late he will be, Mary." "Who?" "Charles." "He is not going, he is not very well to-day," was the reply. Martha thought nothing of it, how should she. Mary buried her fears within her, and said no more. Martha Taylor has had a romance in her life as so many have had. It had partially died out years ago, not quite; its sequel had to come. She sat there listlessly, her pretty hands resting on her knees, her beautiful face tinged with the sunlight—sat there thinking of him—Mark Blakely. A romance it had really been. Martha had paid a long visit to Mrs. Blakely some four or five years before this time. She, Mrs. Blakely, was in perfect health then, fond of gayety, and had many visitors, and before he and Martha knew well what they were about, they had learned to love. He was the first to awake from the pleasant dream, to know what it meant, and he directly withdrew himself out of harm's way. Harm only to himself, as he supposed. He never suspected that the like love had won its way to Martha's heart. A strictly honorable man, he would have killed himself in self-condemnation had he suspected that it had. Not until he had gone did Martha find out that he was a married man. When only nineteen years of age he had been drawn into one of those unequal and unhappy alliances that can only bring a flush to the face in after years. Many a hundred times had it dyed that of Mark Blakely. Before he was twenty he had separated from his wife, when Miss Martha was still a child, and the next six years he traveled on the continent, striving to lose its remembrance. His own family, you may be sure, did not pain him by alluding to it then or after his return. He had no residence in the neighborhood of Bellville. When he visited the town he was the guest of the postmaster, Mr. Hunt. So it happened when Martha met him at his home she never thought of his being a married man. On Mrs. Blakely's part, she never thought that Martha did not know it. Mark supposed she knew it, and when the thought would flash over him, he would say mentally, "how she must despise me for my mad folly." He had learned to love her, to love her passionately, never so much as harboring the thought that it could not be reciprocated—he a married man. But this was no less folly than the other had been, and Mark Blakely had the good sense to leave the place. A day or two after he left his mother received a letter from him. Martha was in her dressing-room when she read it. "How strange," was the comment of Mrs. Blakely. "What do you think, Martha?" she added, lowering her voice. "When he reached Paris there was a note sent to him saying that his wife was dying, and imploring him to come and see her." "His wife," cried Martha; "whose wife?" "My son's; have you forgotten that he had a wife? I wish that we all could really forget it; it has been the blight upon his life." Martha had discretion enough left in that unhappy moment not to betray that she had been ignorant of the fact. When her burning cheeks had cooled a little, she turned from the window where she had been hiding them and escaped to her own room. The revelation had betrayed to her the secret of her own feelings for Mark Blakely, and in her pride and rectitude she thought that she would die. A day or two more and he was a widower. He suffered some months to elapse and then came to Bellville, his object being to visit Martha Taylor. She believed that he meant to ask her to be his wife, and Martha was not wrong. She could give herself up now to the full joy of loving him. Busy tongues, belonging to some young ladies who could boast more wit than discretion, hinted something of this to Martha. She, being vexed at having her private feelings suspected, spoke slightingly of Mark Blakely. "Did they think that she would stoop to a widower, one who had made himself so notorious by his first marriage?" she asked, and this, word for word, was repeated to Mark Blakely; it was repeated to him by those false friends, and Martha's haughty manner as she spoke it offensively commented upon. Mark Blakely, believing it fully, judged that he had no chance with Martha, and, without speaking to her of his intentions, he again left. But now no suspicion of this conversation having been repeated to him ever reached Martha. She considered his behavior very bad. Whatever restraint he had laid upon his manner towards her when at his home, he had been open enough since, and she could only believe his conduct unjustifiable, the result of fickleness. All this time, between two and three years, had she been trying to forget it. If she had received an offer of marriage from a young and handsome man; it would have been in every way desirable; but poor Martha found that Mark Blakely was too deeply seated in her heart for her to admit thought of another. And again Mark Blakely had returned to Bellville, and, as Martha had heard, dined at Mrs. Hunt's, the wife of the postmaster; he had called at her house since his return, but she was out.

She sat there thinking of him, her prominent feeling against him being anger. She believed until this hour that he had treated her mean; that his behavior had been unbecoming a gentleman. Her reflections were disturbed by the entrance of Doctor Brown. It was growing dark then, and she wondered what brought him there so late—in fact, what brought him there at all. She turned and asked the question of Mary. "He has come to see Charles," replied Mary; and Martha noticed that her sister was sitting in a strangely still attitude, her head bowed down; but she did not connect it with the real cause. It was nothing unusual to see Mary lost in deep thought. "What is the matter with Charles, that Mr. Brown should come?" inquired Martha. "He did not feel well and sent for him." It was all that Mary answered, and Martha continued in blissful ignorance of anything being wrong and resumed her reflections on Mark Blakely. Mary saw the doctor before he went away; afterward she went to Charles' room, and remained in it. Martha remained in the dining-room, buried in her dream of love. The rooms were lighted, but the blinds were not closed.

Martha was near the window, looking forth into the bright moonlight. It must have been getting quite late, when she discovered some one approaching their house. She thought at first that it might be her cousin George, but, as the figure drew nearer, her heart gave a great bound, and she saw that it was he upon whom her thoughts had been fixed. Yes, it was Mark Blakely. When he mentioned to Mrs. Hunt that he had a visit to pay to a sick friend, he had reference to Charles Taylor. Mark Blakely, since his return, had been struck with the change in Charles Taylor; it was more perceptible to him than to those who saw Charles habitually, and, when the apology came for Mr. Taylor's absence, Mark determined to call upon him at once, though, in talking with Mrs. Hunt, he nearly let the time for it slip by. Martha arose when he entered; in broad day he might have seen, beyond a doubt, her changing face, telling of emotion. Was he mistaken in fancying that she was agitated? His pulses quickened at the thought, for Martha was as dear to him as she had ever been. "Will you pardon my intrusion at this hour?" he asked, taking her hand and bending towards her with his sweet smile. "It is later than I thought it was—indeed, the hall clock was striking ten! I was surprised to hear of your brother's illness, and wished to hear how he was before I left for home." "He has kept his room this evening," replied Martha. "My sister is sitting with him; I do not think it is anything serious, but he has not appeared very well of late." "Indeed, I trust it is nothing serious," warmly responded Mark Blakely. Martha fell into silence; she supposed that the servant had told Mary that he was there and that she would be in. Mark went to the window. "The same charming scene," he exclaimed; "I think the moonlight view from this window is beautiful, the dark trees around, and these white stone mansions, rising there, remain on my memory like the scene of an old painting." He folded his arms and stood there gazing still. Martha stole a look up at him at his pale, attractive face, with its expression of care. She had wondered once why that look of care was conspicuous there; but not after she became acquainted with his domestic history.

"Are you going away to remain Mr. Blakely," the question awoke him from his reverie, he turned to Martha and a sudden impulse prompted him to address her on the subject nearest his heart. "I would remain if I could induce one to share my name and home. Forgive me, Martha, if I anger you by speaking so hastily; will you forget the past and help me to forget it; will you let me make you my dear wife?" In saying will you forget the past, Mark Blakely alluded to his first marriage in his extreme sensitiveness on that point, he doubted whether Martha would object to succeed the dead Mrs. Blakely, he believed those hasty and ill-natured words reported to him as having been spoken by her, bore on that point alone. Martha on the contrary assumed that her forgetfulness was asked for his own behavior to her in so far that he had gone away and left her without a word of explanation. She grew quite pale with anger. Mark Blakely resumed; his manner earnest, his voice low and tender, "I have loved you Martha from the first day that I saw you at my mother's, I dragged myself away from the place because I loved you, fearing that you might come to see my folly, it was worse than folly then, for I was not a free man. I have continued loving you more and more from that time to this. I went abroad this last time hoping to forget you, but I cannot do it, and my love has only become stronger. Forgive, I say, my urging it upon you in this moment of impulse." Poor Martha was greatly excited, went abroad hoping to forget her, striving to forget her, it was worse and worse. She pushed his hand away. "Oh! Martha, can you not love me?" he exclaimed in agitation. "Will you not give me hopes that you will some time be my wife." "No, I cannot love you; I will not give you hopes. I would rather marry any man in the world than you; you ought to be ashamed of yourself, Mr. Blakely!" Not a very dignified rejoinder, and Martha first with anger and then with love, burst into even less dignified tears, and left the room in a passion. Mark Blakely bit his lips in disgust. Mary entered unsuspicious; he turned from the window and smoothed his brow, gathering what equanimity he could as he proceeded to inquire after Mr. Taylor. About a month after this interview Martha Taylor walked out from the dining-room to enjoy the beauty of the spring evening, or to indulge her own thoughts as might be. She strayed to the edge of the grounds and there sat down on the garden bench, not to remain alone long. She was interrupted by the very man upon whom, if the disclosure must be made, her evening thoughts had centered. He was coming up with a quick step, seeing Martha he stopped to accost her, his heart beating, beating from the quick steps or from the sight of Martha, he best knew. Many a man's heart has beaten at the sight of a less lovely vision. She wore white, set off with blue ribbons, and her golden hair glittered in the sunlight. She nearly screamed with surprise; she had been thinking of him, it was true, but as one who was miles away. In spite of his stormy and not long past rejection, he went straight to her and held out his hand. Did he notice that her blue eyes dropped beneath his as she rose to answer his greeting? that the soft color on her cheeks changed to a hot damask. "I fear I have surprised you," said Mark. "A little," acknowledged Martha. "I did not know you were in Bellville. Charles will be glad to see you."

She turned to walk with him to the house and as in courtesy bound, Mark Blakely offered her his arm, and Martha condescended to accept it; neither broke the silence, and they reached the large porch at the Taylor mansion. Martha spoke then. "Are you going to make a long stay in England?" "A very short one; a party of friends are leaving for New York, and they wish me to accompany them, I think I shall go." "To New York that is a long distance." Mark smiled, "I am an old traveler, you know." Martha opened the dining-room door, Charles was alone, he had left the table and was seated in his armchair by the window, a glad smile illumed his face when he saw Mark, he was one of the very few of whom Charles had made a close friend, these close friends, not more than one or two perhaps, can we meet in a life-time; acquaintances many, but friends, those to whom the heart can speak out its inmost thoughts who may be as our own souls, how few. "Have you been to tea?" asked Charles. "I have dined at the hotel," replied Mark. "Have you come to make a long stay?" inquired Charles. "I shall leave to-morrow, having nothing to do I thought that I would come and see you, I am pleased to see you looking better." "The warm weather seems to be doing me a little good," was Charles Taylor's reply; a consciousness within him of how little better he really was, Charles proceeded with Mark to the drawing-room where his sisters were, and a pleasant hour or two they all spent together.

# VIII

## George Taylor Gives a Party

Matilda laughed at him a great deal about his proposed expedition to New York, telling him she did not believe that he was serious in saying he entertained it. It was a beautiful night, soft, warm and lovely, the clock was striking ten when Mark arose to depart. "If you will wait a few minutes I will go a little way with you," said Charles Taylor, he withdrew to another room for his coat, then he rejoined him, passed his arm in Mark Blakely's and went out with him. "Is this New York project a joke?" asked Charles. "Indeed, no, I have not quite made up my mind to go, I think I shall; if so, I shall go in a week from this, why should I not go, I have no settled home, no ties?" "Should you not, Mark, be the happier if you had a settled home; you might form ties, I think a roving life must be a very undesirable one." "It is one I was never fitted for, my inclination would lead me to love home and domestic happiness, but as you know, I put that out of my power." "For a time, but that is over, you might marry again." "I do not think I ever shall," returned Mark Blakely, feeling half prompted to tell his unsuspicious friend that his own sister was the barrier.

"You have never married," he resumed, allowing the impulse to die away. Charles Taylor shook his head; "the cases are different," he said: "In your wife you lost one whom you could not regret." "Don't call her by that name Charles;" burst forth Mark Blakely. "And in Janey I lost one who was all the world to me who could never be replaced," Charles resumed, after a pause; "the cases were widely different." "Yes, widely different," assented Mark Blakely, they walked on in silence, each buried in his own thoughts, at the commencement of the road, Mark Blakely stopped, and took Charles Taylor's hand in his, "you shall not come any farther with me."

Charles stopped also, he had not intended to go farther. "You shall really go to New York then." "I believe I shall." "Take my blessing with you, then Blakely we may never meet again in this world."

"What!" exclaimed Mark. "The medical men entertain hopes that my life may not be terminated so speedily, I believe that a few months will end it, I may not live to welcome you home." It was the first intimation

SARAH E. FARRO

Mark Blakely had received of Charles fatal malady, Charles explained to him; he was overwhelmed. "Oh my friend! my friend! can not death be coaxed to spare you!" he called out in excitement, how many have vainly echoed the same cry! A few more words, a long grasp of the lingering hands, and they parted, Charles with a God speed, Mark with a different prayer, a God save upon his lips. Mark Blakely turned to the road, Charles towards home. George Taylor's dinner-table was spacious, but the absence of one person from it was conspicuous. Mr. Blakely's chair was still left. "He would come yet." George said there was no clergyman present, and Charles Taylor said the grace, he sat at the foot of the table opposite his cousin.

"We are thirteen!" exclaimed Mr. Feathersmith, a young man of this aristocratic gathering, "it is the ominous number, you know." Some of them laughed. "What is that peculiar superstition?" asked Major Black, "I have never been able to understand it." "The superstition is that if a party of thirteen sit down to dinner one of them is sure to die before the year is up," replied the young man, speaking with grave seriousness. "Why is not thirteen as good a number to sit down as any other number?" cried Major Black. "As good as fourteen, for instance?" "It's the odd number." "The odd number; it's no more the odd number than any other number is odd that's not even. What do you say to eleven? What do you say to fifteen?" "I can't explain it," returned the young man, with an air of indifference. "I only know that the superstition does exist, and that I have noticed in more instances than one that it has been carried out. Three or four parties of thirteen who have sat down to dinner have lost one of their number before the close of the year. You laugh at me, of course. I have been laughed at before; but suppose you notice it now; there are thirteen of us, see if we all are alive at the end of the year." Charles Taylor in his heart thought it not unlikely that one of them, at any rate, would not be living. Several faces were smiling with amusement, the most serious of them was Mark Blakely. "You don't believe in it, Blakely?" cried one, in surprise, as he gazed at him. "I certainly do not, why should you ask it?" "You look so grave over it." "I never like to joke, though it be but a smile, on the subject of death," replied Mark. "I once received a lesson on the point, and it will serve me for life." "Will you tell us what it was?" interposed Mr. Feathersmith, who was introduced to Mr. Blakely that day. "I cannot tell it now," replied Mark. "It is not a subject suited to a merry party," he frankly added, "but it would not tend to bear out your superstition, sir; you are possibly thinking that it might." "If I have sat down once with thirteen, I have sat down fifty times," cried Major Black, "and we all lived the year out and many after that. I would not mention such nonsense again, if I were you." The young man did not answer for a moment, he was enjoying a glass of wine. "Only notice, that's all," said he, "I don't want to act the simpleton, but I don't like to sit down with thirteen." "Could we not make Bell the scapegoat and invoke the evil to fall on his head?" cried a mocking voice. "It is his fault." "Mr. Feathersmith," interrupted another, "how do you estimate the time? Is the damage to accrue before this year is out or do you give us full twelve months from this evening?" "Ridicule me as much as you like," said the young man, good humoredly. "All I say is, notice if every one of us now here are alive this time next year, then I'll not put faith in it again. I hope we shall be." "I hope we shall be, too," said Major Black. "You are a social subject, though, to invite to dinner. I should fancy Mr. George Taylor was thinking so." Mr. George Taylor appeared to be thinking of something that rendered him somewhat mentally disturbed, in point of fact his duties as host were considerably broken into by listening at the door; above the conversation, the clatter of plates, the drawing of corks, his ear was alive, hoping for the knock which would announce Mr. Bell.

It was, of course, strange that he neither came nor sent, but no knock seemed to come and George could only rally his powers and forget him. It was a recherche repast. George Taylor's state dinners always were; no trouble or expense was spared at them; luxuries in season and out of season were there; the turtle would seem richer at his table than any other, the venison more than venison, the turkeys had a sweeter flavor, the sparkling champagne was of the rarest vintage, the dinner this day did not disgrace its predecessors and the guests seemed to enjoy themselves to the utmost in spite of the absence of Mr. Bell and Mr. Feathersmith's prognostications thereon. The evening was drawing on, and some of the gentlemen were solacing themselves with a cup of coffee, when the butler slipped a note into George's hand. "The man is waiting for an answer, sir," he whispered. George glided out of the room and read it, so fully impressed was he that it came from Mr. Bell explaining the cause of his absence that he had to read it twice over before he could take in the fact that it was not from him; it was few lines in pencil from the popular hotel and running as follows: "Dear George, I am not feeling well and have stopped here on my journey, call at once or I shall be gone to bed, Adam Miller." One burning desire

SARAH E. FARRO

had hung over George all the evening that he could run up to Bell's, and learn the cause of his absence. His absence in itself would not in the least have troubled George, but he had a most urgent reason for wishing to see him, hence his anxiety. To leave his guests to themselves would have been scarcely the thing, but this note appeared to afford just the excuse wanting, at any rate he determined to make it the excuse. "A messenger brought this, I suppose," he said to the butler. "Yes, sir." "My compliments and I will be with Mr. Miller directly." George went into the room again, intending to proclaim his proposed absence and plead Mr. Miller's illness which he would put up in a strong light as his justification for the inroad upon good manners a sudden thought came over him that he would only tell Charles. George drew him aside, "Charles, you be host for me for half an hour," he whispered. "Mr. Miller has just sent me an urgent summons to come and see him at the hotel; he was passing through here and was compelled to stop for sickness." "Won't to-morrow morning do?" asked Charles. "No, I will be back before they have time to miss me, if they do miss me, say it is a duty of friendship that any one of them would have answered as I am doing, if called upon. I'll soon be back." Away he went. Charles felt unusually well that evening and exerted himself for his cousin. Once out of the house George hesitated whether he should go to see Mr. Bell or Mr. Miller. He went to Mr. Miller. They had been friends first at school, then at college, and since up to now. "I am sorry to have sent for you," exclaimed Mr. Miller holding out his hand. "I hear you have friends this evening." "It's the kindest thing you could have done for me this evening," answered George. "I would have given anything for a plea to be absent myself, and your letter came and afforded it." What, else they said, was between themselves; it was not much, and in five minutes he was on his way to Bell's; on he strode his eager feet scarcely touching the ground, he lifted his hat and wiped his brow, hot with anxiety; it was a very bright night the moon high; he reached the mansion, and rang the bell: "Is Mr. Bell at home?" "He's gone to the North River," was the answer. "A pretty trick he played me this evening," said George in a tone of dismay. "What trick," repeated the house-keeper. "Gone to North River, it cannot be." "He is," said she positively; "when I came from market, I found him going off by the train he had received a message which took him up."

"Why did he not call upon me, he knew the necessity there was for me to see him, he ought to have come." "I conclude he was in a hurry to catch the train," said she. "Why did he not send?" "I heard him send a verbal message by one of the servants to the effect that he was summoned unexpectedly to North River, and could not, therefore, attend your dinner. How early you have broken up!" "We have not broken up, I left my guests to see after him. No message was brought to me." "Then I will enquire," began she, rising, but George waved her back. "It is of little consequence," he said. "It might have saved me some suspense, but I am glad I got the dinner over without knowing it. I would like to see him." George arose to go. "Not there, not that way," she said, for George was turning as if he would go into a dark hall, and she arose and went with him to the door. He intended to take the lonely road homewards, that dark, narrow road you may remember, where the maple trees met overhead. All at once George Taylor did take a step back with a start, when just inside the walk there came a dismal groan from some dark figure seated on a broken bench. It was all dark there, the thick maple trees hid the moon. George had just emerged from where her beams shone bright and open, and not at first did he distinguish who was sitting there, but his eyes grew accustomed to the obscurity. "Charles," he uttered in consternation, "is that you?" For answer, Charles Taylor caught hold of his cousin, bent forward and laid his head on George's arm, another deep groan breaking from him; that George Taylor would rather have been waylaid by a real ghost than by his cousin at that particular time and place, was certain; better that the whole world should detect any undue anxiety for Mr. Bell's companionship then than Charles Taylor, at least George thought so, but conscience makes the best of us cowards, nevertheless he gave his earnest sympathy to his cousin. "Lean on me Charles, let me support you, how have you been taken sick?" another minute and the paroxysm of pain was past. Charles wiped the moisture from his brow, and George sat down on the narrow bench beside him. "How came you to be here alone, Charles. Where is your carriage?" "I ordered the carriage early and it came just as you were going away," explained Charles. "Feeling well, I sent it away again, saying I would walk home, the pain struck me just as I reached this spot and but for the bench I should have fallen." "But George, what brings you here?" was the next very natural question. "You told me that you was going to see Miller?" "So I was— so I did," said George, speaking volubly. "I found him poorly, I told him that he would do better in bed and came away; it was a nice night; I felt inclined for a run, and went to Bell's to ask what kept him away. He was

SARAH E. FARRO

sent for up at North River it seems, and sent an apology, but I did not get it. In some way or other I think it was misplaced by the servants." Charles Taylor might well have rejoined "If Bell was away where did you stop," but he made no remark. "Are they all gone," asked George, alluding to his guests. "They are all gone, I made it right with them respecting your absence; my being there was almost the same thing, they appeared to regard it so. George, I believe I must have your arm as far as the house, see what an old man I am getting to be." "Will you not rest longer, I am in no hurry as they have gone? What can this pain be that seems to be attacking you of late?" "Has it never occurred to you what it might be?" rejoined Charles. "No," replied George, but he noticed that Charles' tone was a peculiar one, and he began to think of all the ailments that flesh is heir to. "It cannot be rheumatism, can it Charles?" "It is something worse than rheumatism," he said, in his serene, ever thoughtful tone. "A short time George, and you will control my share of the business." George's heart seemed to stand still and then bound onward in a tumult. "What do you mean, Charles; what do you think is the matter with you?" "Do you remember what killed my mother?" There was a painful pause. "Oh, Charles!" "That is it," said Charles quietly. "I hope you are mistaken! I hope you are mistaken!" reiterated George. "Have you a physician; you must have advice!" "I have had it, Brown confirms my suspicions. I asked for the truth." "Who is Brown," returned George, disparagingly. "Go to London, Charles, and consult the best medical men there."

"For the satisfaction of you all I can do so," he replied; "but it will not benefit me." "Good heavens! what a dreadful thing," uttered George, with feeling; "what a blow to fall upon you." "You would regard it so were it to fall upon you, and naturally you are young, joyous, and have something to live for." George Taylor did not feel joyous then, had not felt particularly joyous for a long time; some how his own care was a burden to him; he lifted his right hand to his temple and kept it there; Charles suffered his own hand to fall upon George's left, which rested on his knee. "Don't grieve, George, I am more than resigned. I think of it as a happy change; this world at its best is full of care; if we seem free from it one year it only falls more unsparingly the next; it is wisely ordered, were the world made too pleasant for us, we might be wishing it was our permanent home; few weary of it, whatever may be their care, until they have learned to look for a better. In the days gone by, I have felt tempted to wonder why Janey should have been taken," resumed

Charles. "I see now how merciful the fiat was, George. I have been more thoughtfully observant perhaps, than many are, and I have learned to see, to know, how marvelously all the fiats are fraught with mercy; full of dark sorrows as they may seem to us, it would have been a bitter trial to me to leave her here unprotected in deep sorrow. I scarcely think I could have been reconciled to go, and I know what her grief would have been. All's for the best." Very rare was it for undemonstrative Charles thus to express his hidden sentiments. George never knew him to do so before; the time and place were peculiarly fitted for it, the still, bright night, telling of peacefulness, the shady trees around, the blue sky overhead; in these paroxysms of pain Charles felt himself brought face to face with death. "It will be a blow to Mary," said George, the thought striking him. "She will feel it as one. Charles, can nothing be done for you?" was the impulsive rejoinder. "Could it have been done for my mother?" "I know, but since then science has been broadened; diseases once incurable yield now to medical skill. I wish you would go to London. There are some diseases which bring death with them in spite of human skill, which will bring it to the end of time," rejoined Charles. "This is one." "Well, Charles, you have given me enough for to-night, and for a great many more nights and days, too. I wish I had not heard it; it is a dreadful affliction for you. I must say it is a dreadful affliction." "The disease or the ending you mean?" asked Charles, with a smile. "Both are, but I spoke more particularly of the disease. The disease in itself is a lingering death, and nothing better." "A lingering death is the most favored, as I regard it; a sudden death the most unhappy one. See what time has given me to set my house in order," he added, the sober smile deepening. "I must not fail to do it well." "And the pain, Charles, that will be lingering, too." "I must bear it." He rose as he spoke, and put his arm in his cousin's. He stood a minute or two as if getting strength, and then walked on, leaning heavily on George. It was the pain, the excessive agony, that unnerved him; a little while, and he would seem in the possession of his strength again. "George, I can not tell how you will manage the business when I am gone," he continued, more in a business-like tone. "I think of it a great deal. Sometimes I fancy it might be better if you took a staid, sober partner, one of middle age, a thorough man of business. Great confidence has been accorded me, you know, George. I suppose people like my steady habits."

"They like you for your honest integrity;" returned George, the words seemed to break from him impulsively, "I shall manage very well, I dare say, when the time comes, I suppose I must settle down to business to be more like what you have been, I can," he continued in a sort of soliloquy, "I can, and I will." But they walked on slowly neither saying a word until they reached the house. George shook hands with his cousin, "don't you attempt to come to business to-morrow," he said, "I will come up in the evening to see you."

"Won't you come in now, George?" "Thank you. Good night, Charles, I heartily wish you better." There went on the progress of a few days and another week had dawned and Charles seemed to all appearances to be improving, he arose now to the early breakfast table, he began to hasten to business for there was much work there with the accounts, and one morning when they were at breakfast the old servant entered with one or two letters for Charles, but before the old man could reach his master, whose back was toward the door, Mary made him a sign and he laid the letters down on a remote table. Charles had been receiving a large number of letters of late, and Mary was fearful that so much business might bring on another of those spells and deemed it just as well that he should at least eat his breakfast in peace. The circumstances of the letters having passed from her mind he ate on in silence, but Martha and Matilda were discussing certain news which they had received the previous day, news which had surprised them concerning the engagement of a lady who had looked upon matrimony as folly.

# IX

## CHARLES RECEIVES ANOTHER STROKE

Busy talking they did not particularly notice that Charles had risen from his chair at the breakfast table and was seated at a distant table opening his letters until a faint sound, something like a groan, startled them; he was leaning back in his chair seemingly unconscious, his hands had fallen, his face gave signs of the grave; surely those dews upon it were not the dews of death! Martha screamed, Matilda flung open the door and called out for help; Mary only turned to them her hands lifted to enjoin silence, a warning word upon her lips, their old servant came running in and looked at Charles. "He'll be better directly," he whispered. "Yes, he will be better," assented Mary, "but I should call the doctor." Charles began to revive. He slowly opened his eyes and raised his hand to wipe the moisture from his white brow. On the table before him lay one of the letters open. Mary pushed the letters aside with a gesture of grievous vexation. "It is this business that has affected you," she cried out with a wail. "Not so," breathed Charles. "It was the pain here." He touched himself below the chest in the same place where the pain had been before. What had caused the pain, mental agony arising from overwork or the physical agony arising from disease? Probably some of both. He stretched out his hand toward the letters making a motion that they should be placed in envelopes. George, who could not have read a word without his glasses, took up the letters, folded them and put them in their envelopes. Charles' mind seemed at rest and he closed his eyes again. "I'll step for the doctor now," whispered George to Mary, "I shall catch him before he goes out on his rounds." He took his hat and went down the road to the office, putting forth his best step, when he reached the office the doctor had gone. "Will he be long," asked George? "I don't know," was the reply, "he was called out at seven this morning." "He is wanted at the Taylor mansion. Mr. Taylor is worse." "Is he?" returned the assistant, his quick tone indicating concern. "I can tell you where he is, and that's at Bangs," continued the assistant. "You might call and speak to him if you like, it's on your way home." George hastened there and succeeded in finding the doctor. He informed him that Charles was worse; was very sick. "One of the old attacks of pain, I suppose," said the doctor. "Yes, sir," answered George. "He was taken sick while answering letters. Miss Mary thought it might be overwork that brought it on."

"Ah!" said the doctor, and there was a world of emphasis on the monosyllable. "Well, I shan't be detained here over half an hour longer, and I shall come straight up." He reached there within half an hour after George. Mary saw him approaching and came into the hall to meet him. She was looking very sad and pale. "Another attack, I hear," began the doctor, in his unceremonious mode of salutation, "bothered into it, I suppose; George says it came on while he was reading letters." "Yes," answered Mary, in acquiescence, her tone a resentful one. "It was brought on by overwork." The doctor gave a groan as he turned towards the stairs. "Not there," interposed Mary, "he is in the dining-room." With the wan, white look upon his face, with the moisture of pain on his brow lay Charles Taylor. He was on the sofa now, but he partially rose from it and assumed a sitting posture when the doctor entered. A few professional questions and answers and then the doctor began to scold. "Did I not warn you that you must have perfect tranquility," cried he, "rest of body and of mind?" "You did, but how am I to get it, even now I ought to be at the office. I shall die however it may be, doctor," was the reply of Charles Taylor. "So will most of us, I expect," returned the doctor, "but there's no necessity for us to be helped on to it ages before death would come of itself." "True," replied Charles, but his tone was not a hopeful one. There was a pause, Charles broke it. "I wish you could give me something to avert these sharp attacks of pain, doctor, it is agony in fact, not pain." "I know it," replied the doctor. "What's the use of my attempting to give you anything? You don't take my prescription." Charles lifted his eyes in surprise. "I have taken all that you desired me." "No, you have not; I prescribe tranquillity of mind and body; you take neither." Charles leaned nearer to the doctor and paused before he answered. "Tranquillity of mind for me has passed, I can never know it again; were my life to be prolonged by the great healer of all things, time might bring it to me in a degree, but for that I shall not live, doctor; you must know this to be the case under the calamity which has fallen upon my head." "At any rate you cannot go on facing business any longer." "I must, indeed, there is no help for it." "And suppose it kills you," was the retort. "If I could help going I would," said Charles. "George has gone away." The doctor arose and departed after giving Charles a severe lecture. Miss Taylor sat at one of the west windows, her cheek rested pensively on her fingers as she thought, oh, with what bitterness of the grievous past she sat there losing herself in regret after regret. If my father and mother had not died; she lost herself, I say, in these regrets, bitter as they were vain. How many of these useless regrets might embitter the lives of us all, how many do embitter them? If I had but done so and so; if I had taken the right when I turned to the wrong; if I had known who that person was from the first and shunned his acquaintance; if I had chosen that path in life instead of this one; if I had, in short, done exactly the opposite to what I did do. Vain, vain repinings; vain, useless repinings. The only plan is to keep them as far as possible from our hearts. If we could foresee the end of a thing at its beginning, if we could buy a stock of experience at the outset of life, if we could, in fact, become endowed with the light of divine wisdom, what different men and women the world would see. But we cannot undo the past, it is ours with all its folly, its shortsightedness. Perhaps its guilt, though we stretch out our yearning and pitiful hands to Heaven in their movement of agony, though we wail out our bitter my Lord pardon me! heal me! help me! though we beat on our remorseful bosom and tear away its flesh piecemeal in bitter repentance. We cannot undo the past; we cannot undo it. The past remains to us unaltered, and must remain so forever. Perhaps some idea of this kind of the utter uselessness of these regrets, but no personal remorse attached to her, was making itself heard in the mind of Miss Taylor even through her grief. She had clasped her hands upon her bosom now and bent her head downwards, completely lost in retrospect.

She was aroused by the entrance of Charles. He sat opposite her at the other corner of the window; he appeared to be buried in thought, neither spoke a word; presently Mary arose to leave the room and George met her almost immediately, showing in Mr. Blakely. He hastened forward to prevent Charles from rising. Laying one hand upon his shoulder and the other on his hands he pressed him down and would not let him rise. The slanting rays of the setting sun were falling on the face of Charles Taylor, lighting up its handsome outlines, the cheeks were thinner, the hair seemed scantier, the truthful gray eyes had acquired an habitual expression of pain. Mr. Blakely leaned over him and noted it all. "Sit down," said Charles, drawing the chair which had been occupied by Mary nearer to him. Mr. Blakely accepted the invitation, but did not release the hand. They subsided into conversation, its theme as was natural, the health of Charles and the topics of the day and weather. Charles sat in calmness waiting for him to proceed; nothing could stir him greatly now. Mr. Blakely gave him the outline of the past, of his love for Martha and her rejection of him. "There has been something in her manner of late," he continued, "which has renewed hope within me, otherwise I should not be saying this to you now; quite of late, since her rejection of me, I have observed what I could not describe, and I have determined to risk my fate once more." "But I did not know that you loved Martha." "I suppose not. It has seemed to me, though, that my love must have been patent to the world. You would give her to me, would you not?" "Thankfully," was the warm answer. "The thought of leaving these girls unprotected has been one of my cares. Let me give you one consolation Blakely, that if Martha has rejected you she has rejected others. Mary fancied she had some secret attachment; can it have been concerning yourself?" "If so why has she rejected me?" "I don't know; she has been grievously unhappy since I have been sick, almost like one who had no further hope in life." "What is it, George?" "A message has come from Mrs. Bangs." Charles spoke a word of apology to Blakely and left the room; in the hall he met Martha crossing to it; she went in quite unconscious who was its occupant; he rose to welcome her. A momentary hesitation in her steps, a doubt whether she should not run away again, and then she recalled her senses and went forward. How it went on and what was exactly said or done neither of them could remember afterwards. A very few minutes and Martha's head was resting upon his shoulder; all the mistakes of the past cleared up between them. She might not have confessed to him how long she had loved, all since that long time when they were together at his home, but for her dread that he might think she was only accepting him on account of Charles' days being numbered. She told the truth, that she had loved him and him only all along. "Martha, my dear, what a long misery might have been spared me had I known this." Martha looked down. Perhaps some might have been spared her also. "Would you like to live here?" asked Mark. "Oh, yes; if it can be." "They will be glad to have me set a price on some of these houses around here." Martha's eyelids were bent on her hot cheeks; she did not raise them. "If you like we might ask Mary and Matilda to live with us," resumed Mark Blakely in his thoughtful consideration. "Our home will be large enough." "Their home is decided upon," said Martha shaking her head, "and they will remain in their own home. Mary has an annuity, you know; it was money left to her by mamma's sister, so that she is independent; can live where she pleases; but I am sure she will go to New York on a visit as soon as"—"I understand you Martha; as soon as Charles shall have passed away." The tears were glistening in her eyes. "Do you not see a great change in him?"

"A very great one, Martha; I should like him to give you to me. Will you waive ceremony and be mine at once?" "At once," she repeated, stammering and looking at him. "I mean in the course of a week or two, as soon as you can make it convenient. Surely we have waited long enough." "I will see," murmured Martha, a grave expression arose to Mr. Blakely's face. "It must not be very long, Martha, if you would be mine while your brother is in life." "I will! I will! it shall be as you wish," she answered, the tears falling from her eyes, and before she could make any rejoinder she had hastily quitted him, and standing before the window stealthily drying her wet cheeks, for the door had opened and Charles Taylor had entered the room.

All the neighbors of Bellville lingered at its doors and windows curious to witness the outer signs of Martha Taylor's wedding; the arrangements for it were to them more a matter of speculation than of certainty since various rumors had been afloat and were eagerly caught up, although of the most contradictory character, all that appeared certain as yet, was that the day was charming and the bells were ringing; to keep the crowd back was an impossibility and when the first carriage came, the excitement in the street was great; it was drawn by two beautiful horses, the livery of the postillions and the crest on the panels of the carriage proclaimed it to be Charles Taylor's. Mark Blakely sat inside with Martha, the next carriage contained the sisters and Charles Taylor, the third contained the bridesmaids wearing hats and beautiful gowns, and the others coming up contained the aristocratic friends of the parties concerned; there was a low murmur of sorrow, of sympathy and it was called forth by the appearance of Charles Taylor; it was some little time now since Charles Taylor had been seen in public and the change in him was startling; he walked forward leaning on the arm of George Taylor, lifting his hat to the greeting that was breathed around, a greeting of sorrow meant, as he knew, for him and his blighted life, the few scanty hairs stood out to their view as he uncovered his head, and the ravages of the disease that was killing him were all too conspicuous on his wasted features. "God bless him, he's very near to the grave," who said this among the crowd, Charles could not tell, but the words and their pathos full of rude sympathy came distinctly upon his ear. The Reverend Mr. Davis stood at the altar, he, too had changed, the keen, vigorous, healthy man had now a gray worn look; he stood there waiting for the wedding party; the pews were filled with ladies dressed appropriately for the occasion, and the church was filled with sweet-smelling flowers and their fragrance filled the air; the bridesmaids led the way, then came Martha and Charles Taylor; she wore an elegant gown of white satin, a tulle veil and orange blossoms, diamond ornaments, the gift of the groom—as lovely a bride as ever stood at the altar. Mr. Blakely and Miss Mary Taylor came next; she wore a gray silk of rare modern pattern. The recollection of the wedding service that he had promised to perform for Charles Taylor and Janey Brewster caused the pastor's voice to be subdued now as he read; how had that contemplated union ended; the pastor was thinking it over now. This one was over, the promises made, the register signed and parson Davis stepped before them and took the hand of Martha. "I pray God that your union may be a happy one; that rests in a great degree with you; Mark Blakely, take care of her," her eyes filled with tears, but Blakely grasped his hand warmly and said: "I will! I will." "Let me bless you both, Blakely," broke in the quiet voice of Charles Taylor. "It may be that I shall not see you again."

"Oh! but we shall meet again, you must not die yet," exclaimed Mark Blakely with feverish eagerness. "My friend I would rather part with the whole world, save Martha than with you." Their hands lingered together and separated. They reached the carriage, notwithstanding the crowd pushed and danced around it, the placing in of Martha, and Mark taking his seat beside her, seemed to be but the work of a moment, so quickly was it done, and Mark Blakely, a pleasant smile upon his face, bowed to the shouts on either side as the carriage wended its way through the crowd, not until it had got into clear ground did the postillions put their horses to a canter, and the bride and groom were fairly on their bridal tour. There was more ceremony needed to place the ladies in the other carriages. Miss Taylor's skirts in their extensive richness took five minutes to arrange themselves, ere a space could be found for Charles beside her, the footman held the door for him, the other carriages drove up in order and were driven quietly away, after having been filled with fair ladies and their escorts.

# X

## A Peaceful Hour

In the old porch at Bellville, of which you have read so much, sat Charles Taylor. An invalid-chair had been placed there, and he lay back on its pillows in the beams of the afternoon sun of the late autumn; a warm sunny day it had been. He was feeling wonderously well; almost, but for his ever present weakness, quite well; his fatigue of the previous day, that of Martha's wedding, had left no permanent effects upon him, and had he not known thoroughly his own hopeless state he might have fancied this afternoon that he was approaching convalescence. Not in his looks, pale, wan, ghastly were they, the shadow of the grim implacable visitor, that was so soon to come, was already on them; but the face in its calm, stillness told of ineffable peace. The brunt of the storm had passed. The white walls of the Taylor mansion glittered brightly in the distance, the dark blue sky was seen through the branches of the trees, growing bare and more bare against the coming winter. The warm rays of the sun fell on Charles Taylor. In his hand he held a book from which others than Charles Taylor have derived consolation and courage. "God is love." He was reading at that moment of the great love of God towards those who strive as he had done to live for him. He looked up, repeating the sentence, "He loves them in death and will love them through the never ending ages to come." Just then his eyes fell on the figure of George, their old servant man, who was advancing towards the mansion. Charles closed his book and held out his hand. "You are not going to leave us yet, Mr. Taylor." "I know not how soon it may be George, very long it cannot be; sit down." He stood yet, however, looking at him, disregarding the bench to which he had pointed, stood with a saddened expression and compressed lips. George's eye was an experienced one, and it may be that he saw the picture which had taken up its abode in his face.

"You be going to see my old master and mistress sir," he said dashing some rebellious moisture from his eyes. "Mr. Charles do you remember it, my poor mistress sat here in this porch the very day she died." "I remember it well, George. I am dying quietly, thank God, as my mother died." "And what a blessing it is when folks can die quietly with their conscience, and all about 'em at peace," exclaimed George. "I am on the threshold of a better world, George," was his quiet answer, "one where sorrow cannot enter." George sat for some little time on the bench talking to him, they had gone back in thought to old times, to the illness and death of his mother, to the long gone scenes of the past, whether of pleasure or pain—a past which for us all seems to bear a charm when recalled to the memory which it had never borne; at length George arose to depart, declining to remain longer; Charles was in his armchair seated by the fire as Mary entered the room, his face would have been utterly colorless save for the bluish tinge which had settled there a tinge distinguishable even in the red blaze. "Have you come back alone," asked Charles, turning towards her. "George Taylor accompanied me as far as the head of the street. Have you had your medicine, Charles?" "Yes." Mary drew a chair near to him, and sat down, glancing almost stealthily at him; when this ominous look appears on the human face we do not like to look into it too boldly lest its owner, so soon to be called away, may read the fiat in our own dread countenance, she need not have feared its effects, had he done so, on Charles Taylor. "How are you feeling to night?" somewhat abruptly asked Mary. "Never better of late days; it seems as if ease both of mind and body has come to me." Mary turned her eyes from the fire that the tears rising in them might not be seen to glisten, and exclaimed: "What a misfortune." "A misfortune to be taken to my rest, to the good God who has so loved and kept me here. A few minutes before you came in I fell into a doze and I dreamt I saw Jesus Christ standing by the window waiting for me, he had his hand stretched out to me with a smile, so vivid had been the impression that when I awoke, I thought it was a reality. Death a misfortune! no, Mary, not for me." Mary rang the bell for lights to be brought in, Charles, his elbow resting on the arm of his chair, bent his head upon his hand and became lost in the imagination of glories that might so soon open to him, bright forms were flitting around a throne of wondrous beauty, golden harps in their hands, and in one of them, her harp idle, her radiant face turned as if watching for one who might be coming, he seemed to recognize Janey. A misfortune for the good to die! No.

George Taylor, a cousin to this family, was seated at his desk in the office when his attention was called by a rap at the door. George opened the door, and the old servant came in. "It is all over, sir," he said; his manner strangely still, his voice unnaturally calm and low, as is sometimes the case where emotion is striven to be suppressed. Miss Mary bade me come to you with the tidings. George's bearing was suspiciously quiet, too. "It is very sudden," he presently rejoined. "Very sudden, sir, and yet my mistress did not seem unprepared for it, he took his tea with her, and was so cheerful over it that I began to hope he had taken a fresh turn, my mistress called me in to give directions about a little matter she wanted done to-morrow, and while she was speaking to me, Miss Matilda cried out. We turned round and saw her leaning over my master, he had slipped back in his chair powerless, and I hastened to raise and support him. Death was in his face, there was no mistaking it, but he was quite conscious, quite sensible and smiled at us. 'I must say farewell to you,' he said, and Miss Matilda burst into a fit of sobs, but my mistress kneeled down quietly before him and took his hands in hers and said, 'Charles, is the moment come?' 'Yes, it is come;' he answered, and tried to look round at Miss Matilda, who stood a little behind his chair. 'Don't grieve,' he said, 'I am going on first,' but she only sobbed the more. 'Good by, my dear ones,' he continued, 'I shall wait for you all as I know I am being waited for.' 'Fear?' he went on, for Miss Matilda sobbed out something that sounded like the word. 'Fear, when I am going to God, when I saw Jesus—Jesus—'" George fairly broke down with a great burst of grief, and the tears were silently rolling over the old man's cheeks. "It was the last word he spoke, 'Jesus,' his voice ceased, his hands fell, and the eyelids dropped, there was no struggle, nothing but a long gentle breath, and he died with the smile upon his lips." Cousin George leaned his head on the side of the window to subdue his emotion, to gather the outward calmness that man likes not to have ruffled before the world; he listened to the strokes of the passing bell ringing out so sharply in the still night air, and every separate stroke was laden with its weight of pain.

You might have taken it for Sunday in Bellville, except that Sundays in ordinary do not look so gloomy; the stores were closed, a drizzling rain came down, and the heavy bell was booming out at solemn intervals; it was tolling for the funeral of Charles Taylor. Morning and night from eight to nine had it so tolled since his death, he had gone to his long home, to his last resting-place, and Bellville mourned for him as for a brother. Life wears different aspects for us and its cares and its joys are unequally allotted, at least they appear so to be. One glances up heavily from careworn burdens, and sees others without care basking in the sunshine, but I often wonder whether those who seem so gay whose

SARAH E. FARRO

path seems to be cast on the broad sunshiny road of pleasure whether they have not a skeleton in their closet; nothing but gayety, nothing but lightness, nothing to all appearances, but freedom from care. Is it really so, perhaps with some, a very few. Is it well for those few? Oh, if we could but see the truth when the burden upon us is heavy and pressing. Fellow sufferers, if we could but read that burden aright, we should see how good it is, and bless the hand that sends it. But we never can; we are but mortal; born with a mortal's keen susceptibility to care and pain, we preach to others that these things are sent for their good, we say so to ourselves when not actually suffering, but when the fiery trial is upon us then we groan out in our sore anguish that it is greater than we can bear. The village clock struck eleven and the old sexton opened the doors of the church, and the inhabitants of this beautiful village assembled to see the funeral as it came slowly winding along the street to the sound of the solemn bell; they might have attended him to the grave following unobtrusively, but that was known to be the wish of the family that such demonstration should not be made. "Bury me in the plainest manner possible" had been his directions when the end was drawing near. The hearse and carriages are standing at the mansion; fine horses, with splendid trappings, in modern carriages, have come from the various parts of the country near and distant to show their owners' homage to that good man who had earned their deepest respect through life; slowly the procession reached the church, and the hearse and carriages stopped at it; some of the carriages filed off, and the drivers turned their horses' heads to face the church, and waited still and quiet while the hearse was emptied. The Reverend Mr. Davis stood at the altar, book in hand, reciting the commencement of the service for the burial of the dead, "I am the resurrection and the life," with measured steps slowly following went those who bore the coffin; their heads covered with a black pall, the sisters and their cousin George came next, with their old servants following, thus they entered the church, he remained at the altar, but not reading from it, the church was nearly filled by ones and twos; they had come in, and when all was quiet, he read the history of the life of the deceased in a solemn manner, there was not a dry eye in the audience; the sermon having been finished, they repaired to the grave, the pastor taking his place at the head, and read the service as the coffin was lowered, the mourners stood next to him, and the other friends were clustered around, their heads bent, the drizzling rain beat down upon their bare heads, the doctor came up, unable to attend earlier, he came now at the last moment, just as George Taylor had come years ago to the funeral of Janey Brewster. Did the pastor of Bellville, standing there with his pale face, his sonorous voice echoing over the graves, recall those back funerals, when he over whom the service was now being read had stood as chief mourner? No doubt he did. Did George recall it? The pastor glanced at him once, and saw that he had a difficulty in suppressing his emotion. "I heard a voice from Heaven saying unto me, write from henceforth blessed are the dead which die in the Lord, even so saith the Spirit, for they rest from their labors." So profound was the silence, that every word as it fell solemnly from the lips of the minister might be heard in all parts of the churchyard; if ever that verse could apply to frail humanity, with its unceasing struggle after holiness, and its unceasing failure here, it most surely apply to him over whom it was being spoken. Bend forward, as so many of those spectators are doing, and read the inscription on the plate, Charles Taylor, aged 40 years. Only forty years, a period at which some men think they are beginning life, it seemed to be an untimely death, and it would have been, after all his pain and sorrow, but that he had entered upon a better life.

They left him in the vaulted grave, his coffin near his mother's, who lay beside his father; the spectators began to draw unobtrusively away, silently and solemnly. In the general crowd and bustle, for everybody was on the move, George turned to the pastor and shook hands with him. "It was a peaceful ending." George was gazing down dreamily as he spoke the last words; the pastor looked at him. "A peaceful ending! yes; it could not be otherwise with him." "No, no," murmured George; "Not otherwise with him." "May God in his mercy send us all as happy a one when our time shall come." As the words left the pastor's lips the loud and heavy bell boomed out again, giving notice to the town that the last rites were over, that life had closed forever on Charles Taylor.

# A Note About the Author

Sarah E. Farro (1859–c. 1937) was an African American novelist. Born to parents who moved from the south the Chicago, Farro was raised alongside two younger sisters and was listed on the 1880 census as "Black." Not much is known about her life, but she was the first African American woman—and the fourth African American—to publish a novel in the nineteenth century. *True Love: A Story of English Domestic Life* (1891), her only novel, was published by Chicago's Donohue & Henneberry and was exhibited at the World's Columbian Exhibition in the city in 1893. Praised at a celebration of pioneering Black Americans in 1937, Farro has largely been forgotten by readers and the public at large. Recently, however, scholars have sought to recognize her outstanding literary achievement.

# A Note from the Publisher

Spanning many genres, from non-fiction essays to literature classics to children's books and lyric poetry, Mint Edition books showcase the master works of our time in a modern new package. The text is freshly typeset, is clean and easy to read, and features a new note about the author in each volume. Many books also include exclusive new introductory material. Every book boasts a striking new cover, which makes it as appropriate for collecting as it is for gift giving. Mint Edition books are only printed when a reader orders them, so natural resources are not wasted. We're proud that our books are never manufactured in excess and exist only in the exact quantity they need to be read and enjoyed.

# Discover more of your favorite classics with Bookfinity™.

- Track your reading with custom book lists.
- Get great book recommendations for your personalized Reader Type.
- Add reviews for your favorite books.
- AND MUCH MORE!

Visit **bookfinity.com** and take the fun Reader Type quiz to get started.

Enjoy our classic and modern companion pairings!